Editing: **Paige Smith**
Cover Design by **Enchanting Romance Designs** www.EnchantingRomanceDesigns.com
Proof: **Amanda Rash**
www.drafthouseeditorialservices.com

Printed in the United States of America

DebraAnastasia.com

FLICKER

DEBRA ANASTASIA

For T, J and D, it's always all for you.
(20th book this time!)

CHAPTER 1

MONDAY

I flipped the switch to high speed so I could cross my eyes. I was settled in bed, my favorite plug-in vibrator nestled in my lady bits, riding the speed train to O-town when the power tool blew the fuse for everyone that had the misfortune of living in my apartment complex.

As I panted in the dark, lightly humping my now dormant love pulser, a fire sparked in the distance. The flames on the pole outside sparked my concern.

I was not surprised that there was an electrical malfunction involving me. I *was* surprised I wasn't dead, or at least twitching from an electrical shock. I knew I was taking risks when I used four old strands of fairy lights connected as a makeshift extension cord. Sure, they were pretty and set a nice mood, but the lights themselves got warm to the touch after being on for a spell. And I had been spelling for a while. It had to be a horrible combination. I strongly felt the farther away from the outlet, the safer I was.

As I crawled over my contraption, I wondered if other residents in the complex were participating in a ménage à moi as well. Rub one out to see the new year in right. Maybe enough to warrant the current situation with our power current. Or if it was just me. It was probably just me.

I wondered if the manager would come knocking to see if we were all okay. Or more importantly to him, if the building was okay.

"Ah shit, I bet it was a squirrel."

One of my neighbors was taking a guess as he walked down the stairs outside. He didn't know I had a dicey vibrator situation. Well, maybe he did. Because of the one time I did myself so right, the wand dropped out of my hand and vibrated on the hardwood floor for about five minutes before I could get my wits about me to turn it off. That had to be a very distinct sound.

But the squirrel bit had me rushing to the closet to put real clothes on. Well, the realest, quickest clothes I could manage by the light of my opened laptop.

I was worried about Mr. Nuts. I jammed a t-shirt that said *every zoo is a petting zoo if you're not a little bitch* on it and baggy sweats. My coat was waiting on a hook by the front door, so I manipulated my hands through the sleeves while cramming my feet into boots.

Mr. Nuts was a sweet friend I was feeding on my porch. When I moved in a few months ago, he came with the property. Clearly, the person before me took to feeding him. Once he and I agreed on his favorite treats, peanuts, I made sure I had them ready for him in the morning.

I ran down the stairs to join the gathering of other curious residents in the parking lot.

The truck from Hanning Electric Company forced all of us to back up. I was pretty sure the driver had just rolled over Mr. Nuts' dead body. I gasped.

When he exited the truck, my sadness and rage were released. I stormed up to him as fast as I could in my UGG boots. "How dare you run him over!"

I slapped the center of his chest. The man was startled and grabbed my wrists. "Who?"

Worry flooded his features while he looked around.

I tried to point at the steaming pile of wildlife. "Mr. Nuts! My squirrel!"

The electric man was taller than I was, and had no trouble keeping me from beating his chest again. He leaned around me to examine the damage. "That's a chipmunk. Well, it *was* a chipmunk."

"What?" I pulled my hands away and turned, looking closer at the corpse I was trying not to see too closely.

"It's a chipmunk." He watched me with one pierced eyebrow lifted.

"How can you tell?" I dropped my gaze to the man's lips. Full with a pair of viper bite rings in the bottom one. He could pass as a celebrity he was so traffic-stopping gorgeous.

"I see a lot of this on the job. Number one reason to lose a transformer is small wildlife getting into things that they shouldn't." He tilted his head, watching to see how I would take his logic.

"So, you're like a Disney Grim Reaper?" I stepped backward and cuddled my boobs.

I breathed a sigh of relief. I was still sad that a chipmunk hadn't survived, but at least it wasn't Mr. Nuts in a crumpled pile.

After telling the residents to back up, the electric man started unpacking his gear. He told them the transformer blew, but it had burned itself out. It was no longer about to burst into a fiery inferno.

I was freezing. Super cold. I looked down at the chipmunk. I was a sucker for animals. I had empathy for the smoking body.

3

Not even thirty minutes had passed since it was out here doing whatever chipmunks did in the middle of the night before I somehow killed him with my vibrator.

I had to do something. I was slightly afraid of the electric man, and I wanted a few steps back from him as well.

Electricity scared me for good reason. I'd been shocked many times in my life. Not to death or anything, but I still hated it. I turned to run back into my apartment. Luckily, the complex had backup safety lights on the stairwell.

BEAR

I watched as the stunning, angry girl rushed from the scene. She was something else. I was so distracted while I was checking her out that I ran over the little rodent that was smoking in the snow. Kind of a gory way to roll up on a job.

But, in my defense, she was a freaking smoke show, too. As she ran back to the building, I started assessing the situation.

I was in the electric business because my dad was and my granddad had been. In my house, the tools of the trade often-times lived on my kitchen counter. No one ever asked me if I would be an apprentice, it just came along with my everyday life.

As of four weeks ago, the family business, Hanning Electric, was now mine to run. Dad was incapacitated with a heart attack. The bad news was, as a small business owner, he didn't have the best health care, so I put my other career on hold to make sure that money would still come in for my parents. Which brought me to being on call on New Year's Eve, and currently standing by a smoking chipmunk. As I set up the ladder after checking that the power was turned off from the main, movement in my peripheral vision made me turn my head.

The woman was back again. Clutched in her mittened hands was a spatula.

Now, I was fully interested in seeing which way this was going to turn. I'd heard rumors of people trying to eat the charred remains of animals on the job, calling it a free barbeque, but I always thought that was an urban legend.

She seemed to be ignoring me completely, her head bowed. I made sure my ladder was sturdy and clipped my tool belt on while she remained silent. I was about to ask her to step back a little when she made the sign of the cross in front of her.

And then she knelt down close to the chipmunk carcass and started hacking away at the snow and ice.

"Um. Are you okay?" I was wondering if she was experiencing some weird sleepwalking or side effects from a drug.

She looked up from her ineffective chopping. "Yeah. I just wanted to bury him. I mean, I'm sure he didn't intend for his night to end like this."

"With a spatula?" I pointed at her hands with my screwdriver.

"I don't have a shovel." She sat back on her heels, looking defeated.

I swallowed my slightly callous laughter. It'd take her a long damn time to make a hole big enough for the chipmunk. It'd take anyone a long damn time to make a decent hole with a kitchen tool in this frozen soil.

"Listen, I'll take him and bury him in a good spot later. It's thirty-three degrees out here." I stepped to the back of my truck and yanked open the rear doors. I had a box of connectors that was just about the right size. I slipped the plastic knobs into a Ziploc bag and held out the box to her.

Her deep brown eyes went from the box to the chipmunk and back again. She didn't want to touch it, I was gathering. I had my work gloves on, so I hollowed out the soon-to-be coffin and plucked the chipmunk's body out of the snow and laid him in the box, folding it closed.

She stood up and narrowed her eyes at me. "You're not just going to toss him out, are you?"

Her rose-colored lips were full, and she bit them together while she ascertained my trustworthiness.

"I've got a place in the backyard that has pets from over the years. He could go there." I put the box next to my father's well-worn wrenches.

"Okay."

The woman seemed to weigh her very limited options.

We stared at each other. Her gaze darted around my face, taking in my piercings. She looked wholesome. Like a true honey and milk farm girl.

"Do you think something caused the transformer to catch fire?" She folded her arms under her breasts and rubbed the sleeves of her coat vigorously to stave off the chill in the air.

It was a bit odd that she'd want the inner workings of the pole in this ice-cold weather.

"Depends. The electric company is on its way. It deals with the pole and the wires to the complex. My dad has a contract with the owners, so I want to see if there's been any damage. Make sure it's safe and all."

"So, you fight electricity?" Her lips parted like she was asking me a sensual question.

"Sort of?" I'd never heard it referred to in that manner, but I was getting turned on by her facial expression.

"That's awesome. Okay. I'm going back up to my place. Thank you for fighting for us. I really appreciate it. And for burying Oscar." She held out her hand formally.

I slipped off one glove to accept the gesture. "You're welcome. It's just my job. And you named him already?"

"Yes. Every soul deserves a name. I'm Monday Blue, by the

way. And you're Harry?" She tilted her head toward the embroidery on my jacket.

"No. Bear. This is my father's jacket. He just had..." I realized I was standing near a ditch, not really the time to tell a stranger about my dad's health problems. "He had to take tonight off. So I'm pitching in. Technically, I'm Harry Junior, but everybody calls me Bear." Her hand was so cold it almost felt like it was fake. "You better get inside."

She took her released hand and jammed it into her jacket pockets.

"Hopefully, I'll be able to get the power on soon." I put my glove back on.

"That's exciting. Okay. I will. Thanks, Bear." And then she hit me with a megawatt smile. I felt my balls literally levitating, my physical reaction to her happiness was so visceral. She gave me miracle balls.

I watched her walk all the way back to the complex, her hips swinging. Monday Blue was hotter than the spark that had killed the chipmunk.

CHAPTER 2

MONDAY

I used the flashlight on my keyring to get around inside of my apartment. Everything always looks different, more ominous without the lights. I had a tricky relationship with electricity. I knew I needed it to survive comfortably in my life, but it also hated me. I found my fluffiest blanket and my phone and curled up on the couch to wait for Bear to do his work.

Bear. Sweet heavens. He was a piece of man candy wrapped in a coat. I googled his company and found his social media page. Harry's wife, Linda, proudly announced that their son would be covering for Harry until he was on the mend. It didn't mention from what, though. The comments below the encouraging photos of his recovery hinted at concerns about electrical jobs being completed.

My apartment complex illuminated, and various beeps and machine noises blurped to life as things for everyone but me came online. I walked to the front windows, and yep, everyone was back in the electrical business except me. In the distance I heard the sound of various doors closing. Because I had not much else to do, I watched as Bear parked below my place. I was three floors up. I had thought being forced to walk up the outdoor stairs would be good exercise, but I hadn't taken into account moving in, or grocery shopping and having to tow all the purchases up from the car when I made that decision.

Bear looked up at my apartment and then headed for the stairs. He was going to be in my place soon. I panic-ran in a circle, and then he was knocking on the door. I flipped the lock and swung it open.

He smiled at me while offering, "Still feeling in the dark?"

His white teeth were straight and framed by two gorgeous come-fuck-me dimples.

"Oh. Yeah. Looks like everyone else is back at full power. You here to turn me on?" I stepped back to allow him room to move past me.

He bit his tongue and ignored the "turn me on" question. He reached out and touched my front door. "This is awesome. Did you do this?"

My door painting. It was a winter scene and even had Mr. Nuts in one of the trees. "Yeah. Hard for me to walk past a fresh canvas."

"Your door? How does management feel about it?" He was still smiling. It was two a.m. on New Year's Eve, and he was smiling. Thank beejesus. Because his smile was a panty incinerator. If I were wearing panties. Which I wasn't. Because of all the lady pleasure I had been partaking in... oh God. I forgot that I had my vibrator plugged in. There wouldn't be a need for him to go into my bedroom, so it's totally cool.

BEAR

Something obviously happened to this apartment's wiring when the transformer blew. Or Monday had a very coincidental problem with her electricity. It wouldn't be very tactful to ask if her payment was up to snuff, so I asked to see her electric panel —normally located in the hallway.

"Sure. This way." Monday led me to the panel, but again, each apartment was a very similar version of each other, so I wasn't surprised.

Her apartment smelled nice. Like very girly with a touch of homey. I was excited to get the lights on here so I could tell if there was a male presence.

Monday seemed a little nervous, and in the beam of my flashlight, I saw her look toward the primary bedroom. Maybe there was a dude in there after all. I put my flashlight between my teeth and opened the fuse box. The fuses were tripped, so something went down in the apartment to force them off. I flipped them back on.

Her place came alive with color. There were so many paintings and art all over the place. She'd painted doorframes and the ceiling, too.

"Damn."

She closed one eye as I cursed. "Yeah. I have an addiction to adding color to the world. I don't think I'll get my security deposit back."

There was a low hum coming from her bedroom. I recognized it immediately as a light bulb that had way too much wattage for the outlet handling it. It was going to blow the fuses again, or worse, explode. I ran past Monday into her bedroom.

There were numerous strings of blinky lights acting as an extension cord for a high-powered vibrator. It was set to the fastest speed, which was imitating an exploding bulb perfectly.

Monday pushed around me and jumped onto the bed, switching off the vibrator as the lights strobed to a flash setting.

"Um."

Her face was beet red. She had been masturbating when the power went out. Well, that was my guess. We couldn't pretend that the vibrator was for a deep muscle massage because it was a very realistic silicone replica extension of a penis.

I put my flashlight in my pocket and took off my hat to scratch my head. "That's not a safe extension cord for" —I pointed from the dick to the wall and back—"...what you were trying to accomplish here."

"Yeah." Monday tossed the dick off the side of the bed. "I have a superstition that the farther away you are from the actual outlet, the safer you are."

I was instantly hard. Possibly visible-from-the-outside-kind of hard. I twisted my hips to point my problem toward the door. "That's super not true at all."

The contract with these apartments was huge for my dad, so I had to get the hell out of here. This looked improper on all accounts, and there was a clause in the contract that forbade my dad from any sexual contact with the residents, which over a year ago had made us all laugh. Mom and Dad had been married for over thirty-five years. He wouldn't dream of cheating on her. They adored one another.

But me, on the other hand, I could be sexual from time to time.

I hightailed it out of the apartment without saying another word, counting on the cold to slap my dick's aspirations right in his face.

I closed Monday's front door behind me. My dick was barely affected by the weather. Asshole. I had to clear my head a few seconds before I could figure out what to do next.

Finally, I realized getting her a new extension cord was the most important service I could offer. Well, the one that made any reasonable sense. I'd be happy to be her non-plug-in-able dick, but Monday and I had just met. And it wasn't even a date. I was her service person at the moment.

I hustled down to the truck and back when I secured a nice six-foot extension cord from my stock. It was amazing how many problems could be solved with a little more electrical slack. I hesitated outside her colorful door. Instead of knocking, I draped the coil of cord around her doorknob. I wanted to dial down the creep factor as much as possible since I had just seen a very private setup.

After I was happy that the cord was staying put, the door swung open. Monday was still flushed from her blush.

"Oh. Okay. Thanks. How much is this?" She pulled the extension cord off.

"It's free. I want you to be safe. Doing whatever you...uh... need to." So much for avoiding seeming like a creep. I tried to pile on more words to erase the awkwardness. "Unless the light strings are part of it. Some people really like mood setting. Well..." I tapered off as I watched her close her eyes and she cringed with her whole body. "Sorry. Sorry about that. Just... there's the cord. Happy New Year."

Monday opened one eye and gave me a strangled, "You, too," before closing the door. I could've sworn I heard her sliding down on the other side.

I backed away from her door. I had a feeling she and I were going to have at least one thing in common tonight—we each were going to be our own dirty handshake.

CHAPTER 3

MONDAY

I held the extension cord as I sat on the floor. Leave it to me to be caught doing the one thing I never wanted to be caught doing. Figures. And, of course, it was electricity related.

I glared at the outlets. One of my very first memories ever was licking my finger and sticking it in the hole I'd been warned away from by my nanny. I think that was the gateway shock. I invited electricity into my system. And as I sat there, my little kid brain tried to process the feeling of the electricity. After I was released from the alternating current, I couldn't decide if the sensation I'd experienced was hot or cold, so I licked my finger again and went for a second go-round.

Still couldn't decide, it turned out. But I didn't like it. So you'd think I'd be able to avoid dancing with that particular nemesis in the future. But that first set of interactions made electricity and me attracted to each other. Maybe I was the only one that had willingly been shocked twice. And like a loyal dog, electricity was trying to follow me around.

We had plenty of outlets in my house. I had to call it a house because there were stringent rules to qualify as a mansion. Pretty sure my mother's insistence on that correction every damn time was to give my dad the business. Mom was ridiculous. Hell, even her first name was ridiculous—Chestnut. Her actual name on her birth certificate was Chelsey. She insisted the world call her Chestnut because she was convinced it sounded richer. It was all about how things looked. I think she wanted to call her house a mansion. We only had six thousand square feet on the Hudson River. My sisters and I had our own wing with two bathrooms and a toy room.

Dad's business was always a murky kind of situation. We had money, but Mom wanted more. She wanted prestige and hereditary money that was too much to spend in one lifetime. Too much to ever accumulate in one lifetime even.

Dad was the director of maintenance for the school system. Great for paying bills and providing, but our last name, Level, would never be etched into a placard neatly centered above a wing of a hospital. Mom aspired to reach a contingent of rich that only few ever saw in their lifetime. Unfortunately for her, a few of her friends were among those few.

Callous schoolmates called Dad a trashman. There were a ton of things involved in his job. The personnel making sure the schools were sparkling and safe were under his direction. His recycling pile was a fountain of inspiration for me. He always brought home odd-looking boxes and handfuls of beads when I was little. As I grew older, he brought bushels of canvases for me and even arranged for me to paint a mural in a preschool. Dad could paint as well, but he was given a job as the head of maintenance at a middle school right out of high school by my grandfather because Mom was pregnant with Lottie.

Later in my school career, I heard whispers about being the

trashman's daughter. My sisters took it to heart, but I shrugged it off. Maybe it was the creative side of me—being able to turn off the real world and delve into my imagination that protected me from the taunting.

Dad could have been a painter in a different life, and I was living his dream as an art teacher. But Mom was another story. She had three daughters. We each had a responsibility to marry a rich husband, so the man could take care of our parents in their retirement. Mom wanted social connections, too. Invitations to the exclusive parties she hadn't received yet. There was no need to feel like Mom was left out, though—she had a circle of friends that my sisters and I called The Wake, which was also what you called a group of vultures that were feeding on a carcass together. Lottie was the first one married. She was the most like Mom, so the expensive suits that Brent, her husband, wore called to her. Brent was shifty about where he worked and called himself an entrepreneur. And he was. He manufactured bullshit better than anyone else, he could probably trademark it. Luckily, Lottie was hard-headed and determined, so she started selling fake essential oils. Unfortunately, Brent used her money to try his next scheme. Currently, he was looking into organic silk flowers.

Teva was the middle child. She resembled a combination of my dad and mom. She's dating a football player—second string, but still professional. They traveled a lot together, and I had to blame Mom for insisting if Teva left Daire's side he would cheat on her.

They went to every strip mall and car dealership in the off-season to sign merchandise together. Daire was basically her career. Well, babysitting his penis was.

And then the youngest was me. Monday Blue. I was the unplanned one. So I owed her the most. She'd tell me that I was prettier than my sisters, so I had to score the best husband. It wasn't true. My sisters looked very different from me, but they were stunning in a classic way. I thought my brown eyes were too big and my butt was too...there. But as I came into my adult-hood, society's definition leaned in my body type direction. The very girls that made fun of my ass in high school were now sporting fake ones bigger than mine.

Dad was secretive with me, making sure I knew that he would pay for art school and my teaching degree. He insisted I was too sweet, and Mom was a steamroller. So he fostered some of my independent choices.

But I also wanted to see my mother's eyes sparkle. There was a part of me that was a people pleaser. Maybe it was because I was the youngest. I liked to see all the people I loved smiling. So I had agreed when Mom set me up on a date with her friend's son. He worked in the stock market, easily tossing around Wall Street-isms with impressive frequency.

I liked seeing my mother delight over Poncy Nutwell's family connections and his ability to hold his own in a room full of prestigious cigar smoking businessmen. It all made him her ideal son-in-law. She fawned over him and his very meticulous name brand style. Poncy and I began dating at the end of the summer of my college graduation. I was not thinking about marriage.

I applied to quite a few school districts for art teaching posi-tions, but they were not nearly as plentiful, with each school only having one, or sometimes two schools to one teacher. I was called for an interview here in Midiville when they had a late opening. And now I'd been at Treasure Elementary for one month. Poncy was furious that I was willing to work three hours away from him. I promised I was just getting some lines on my resume, beefing up my experience. He was a bit dramatic for having just started our relationship, but I was taking his anger as a compliment. He wanted to see more of me. And that was a good thing. At least that's how my mom had framed it.

He hadn't visited my new apartment yet, and he actually had

had a tee time scheduled with his work friends so he couldn't help my sister Lottie and me move my furniture in. Tee times to the exclusive club our families were a part of were hard to come by.

Lottie complained the whole time, but she could lift a dresser end like a beast, so we got it done.

As I held my extension cord, I listened to Bear's footsteps slap on the staircase. Well, that would be the end of that. At least I wouldn't have to see him in person again so I could relive the moment we both looked at my festive silicone setup.

I cleaned up after myself and tucked the new cord into my dresser drawer with Veiny, the name of my vibrator. My best friend, Radia, a real estate agent who told me about the listing in Midiville, was going to make fun of me pretty hard on our Face-Time chat tomorrow. Hell, she was the one that bought me Veiny in the first place. She was the one friend in my life that I was totally okay with sharing the weird stuff with. Anything goes for Radia and me. When we met at camp in middle school, she was the cook's daughter who got to attend the pricey place for free as part of her mom's paycheck. We understood each other on a level that seemed telepathic when we were young. Even though she still lived in my old town, we stayed in contact.

CHAPTER 4

BEAR

*A*fter walking into my parents' place, I went to the
kitchen to deposit the groceries I'd bought for them. I
got to the store early. I had no hope of falling asleep after
meeting Monday. The produce that needed to be kept cold, I
put in the crisper. The frozen foods went into the freezer. I put
the bags in the recycling and listened carefully. Mom hadn't
come down the stairs, which she normally did when she heard
me knocking around.

I went up the stairs as quietly as I could. It was super tran-
quil. Mom was lying on top of the comforter and Dad was on
his back. They were holding hands. They will be married thirty-
six years next week.

To say the last month since Dad's heart attack was emotional
was an understatement. Dad had been doing physical therapy
ever since the angioplasty to clear his arteries. Mom was dedicated to being at my father's side. The two of them were very
much a team and the progress was stunning.

They'd changed everything they ate. Each menu for the day was chock-full of veggies and protein. But certain facts had to be faced. Dad's business was their only means of support. And now, they were tapped out of their retirement funds to pay for Dad's procedures. The insurance paid a lot, but the leftover out-of-network costs were astronomical. It was a whole extra job facing the paperwork.

My dreams and hopes of a career were put on hold. Had to be. My parents took care of me all my life, and there was no way I was watching the world kick them when they were down.

I'd stayed with my parents so many times in the last month that I was sure my work had a thick coating of dust on it. Instead of helping Dad part-time, I helped Mom navigate their bills and keep a journal of procedures and doctors. I was meticulous with the documentation. Mom and Dad were my only family and I recognized the need to have all hands on deck.

Seeing them asleep was adorable. I knew they had planned on staying up to kiss at midnight as the new year arrived, but mid-morning napping was unusual. I cleared my throat and Mom's eyes popped open.

She looked confused so I supplied, "You guys fell asleep?"

"Oh yes. Bear! Happy New Year! How'd you do?" She got out of the bed and turned to my father. He was still napping. She felt his forehead and then kissed his cheek. Then she tucked an afghan around him.

She motioned for me to follow while touching her index finger to her lips. When we got to the kitchen, she hugged me and patted my back. "Thank you so much for the groceries."

"Of course. No physical therapy today?" I helped Mom put the gluten-free crackers on the top shelf of the pantry.

"Oh no, he has the day off for New Year's. I'm his therapist. We can get into it later—before dinner. He really did a great job yesterday and I'm proud."

"Well, good on you for learning those fancy things, Mom.

Maybe you can get a PT business started." I opened the fridge and made a snack plate of grapes and cheese to tide us over.

"Tell me about the business we actually do have. You had a late call?" Mom sat with me and popped a grape into her mouth.

"Were you watching Dad's phone? I told you not to check it." I gave her a slightly disappointed look, but I knew she was paying attention to too much of the goings on in Dad's business.

"It made a noise. I wanted to make sure you were okay."

I had the work calls routed to my phone, but the text messages went straight to Dad's. It was a glitch I hadn't figured out how to fix yet. And yes, I recognized the irony of an electrician getting baffled by an electronic.

"It was a transformer down at the Stormfire Estates."

"Squirrel or chipmunk?" Mom started on the gouda cheese.

"What do you think?" She knew the business well.

"Well, your father would say it was a freaking squirrel. They're the worst." Mom sat back in her chair, putting her slippered feet up onto the center support of the table.

"It was a chipmunk. Who woulda guessed?" I felt a smile creep on my face, thinking of Monday's friend Mr. Nuts.

"That's a smile I haven't seen in a while. What's her name?" Mom patted my hand.

I rolled my eyes. "I don't have a specific smile for ladies."

"I'm your mother. You have a special smile for girls. A special smile for your art. A special smile when you were gassy. I know them all."

"This is great information. Thanks." I filled my mouth with a few grapes so maybe she would get distracted from asking me any more questions. Of course, she waited me out.

"Her name?"

I knew my mother. She never did anything halfway. She learned how to help Dad with his PT almost instantaneously. A quick learner, when other people in her generation were flummoxed by all the new technology like cell phones and computers, Mom always seemed hungry for more information. So I knew she would do an internet search on Monday in a hot minute. And with a name like Monday, I was guessing she was super easy to access, but I wanted to be the one to find that out first.

"A few, actually. I saw a few pretty girls last night. So that's the smile." I looked at the floor. I didn't want her mom eyes seeing right through me. Because literally that's all Monday really was. Pretty and sweet with a healthy sexual appetite.

"That's good. You're looking. That means you're headed in the right direction since the breakup with Ella."

Mom moved the conversation to her favorite series on Netflix, leaving me alone with my memories of Ella. Which were mostly horrible. She had been a toxic person. A drainer. An energy vampire. It was a hard breakup because we had been together for so long. I found out she cheated on me, even though we'd been dating since middle school. I had a monogamous heart. It was the way I was built. Like my parents.

Ella and I had stayed together all through high school and college, although the latter was a long-distance situation. It wasn't until after I found out she was cheating by seeing her in a local bar with another dude that I found out more. And there was so much more. It was common knowledge that she was seeing other guys. In college especially. It seemed like she got off on saying she had someone and cheating on them anyway.

Maybe I was her special fetish. It had done some damage. Some deep, painful damage. My friends told me to move on and that I would have no issues dating. Or even screw the dates— just hit it and quit it. Tinder my love life for a few years. But I was a romantic at heart. I wanted to hold hands and hug and make love, not play games that ended in shredded hearts. Speaking of hearts, Mom stood up and said that Dad was awake. She had hearing like a bat.

21

As she hurried upstairs, I pulled out my ringing phone. Mr. Winfred was on the other end.

"Hanning Electric."

I was terrified that someone had reported that I'd been in Monday's apartment looking at her dick vibrator with the blinky lights. How someone would know other than Monday, I wasn't sure, but my nervous system was a hyper asshole.

"Hey, Bear. Thanks for handling that transformer situation."

"No worries, that's what we're here for." I made sure to make my pronoun plural. I wanted everyone to assume that Dad was very hands-on, even if he wasn't at this moment in time. My job was making sure to maintain great reviews for Hanning Electric.

"We had one resident whose apartment was offline, but she said you fixed it?"

I carefully considered my answer. I wasn't sure if he was just curious or if he'd framed the question as a way to trick me. Had Monday complained? I mean, I hadn't meant to see her vibrator.

"Ugh, yeah. It was just a popped fuse. It's back on." I left some silence to invite him to add details or accusations—however this conversation was intended to go.

"Yeah. It makes me nervous..."

I felt my eyes get really big as he paused.

"That maybe there are some faulty fuses. Can you inspect them all and make sure everything looks safe? Nothing like bad publicity of an entire building burning down."

I added silently, "And people possibly being hurt or killed." I wasn't going to lose this contract for Dad, even though that had to be the most callous way I'd ever heard for anyone to ask about safety.

"For sure. I'll be there in a few." I was getting ready to hang up.

Dad walked into the room, Mom under his arm, both looking at me quizzically.

"Oh, wait a minute, do you usually charge extra for a holiday, or is it in the contract?" Mr. Winfred asked.

Dad shook his head slowly. "I'll have to check on it. That's a great question."

The last thing I wanted him to do was look around in his files. I held up my hand.

"I want to make sure everyone is safe, too. I'll pop by and look over each one free of charge. Please do let them know I'll be stopping by. Hanning Electric wants you satisfied."

My tough father nodded once. He approved of my answer— the only thing he could hear from his side. And then his eyes filled a little, and he said, "Thanks, son," as I hung up the phone.

"Absolutely, Dad. Anytime." I gave him his New Year's hug carefully, his big body far more frail since the heart attack.

I was trying not to think about it, but I'd have to see Monday again. And then I smiled. Mom gave me a huge wink, reminding me never to play poker with her in the future.

CHAPTER 5

MONDAY

*E*lectricity. When I was walking back from a friend's house, maybe ten years old, we had a sudden thunderstorm. Only a person who has lived in the mountains can understand what a life-threatening situation that can be. It wasn't *if* lightning would hit but when. And, of course, where. The half-mile walk from my friend's place to mine was normally filled with skipping and trying to catch ladybugs.

The thunderstorm started with a crack and darkening that happened so fast it would have been a joke if it hadn't made me scream.

I could feel the lightning coming. The electricity in the air was untamed. Like a tiger headed at me. Like a wave forming behind me.

I ran. I ran like I could outrun the bolt. God bless hysterical strength. But I was ten and my legs were short. I felt my hair lifting away from my scalp. Like I'd jumped into the water, but there was no water. Only my feet, sending gravel from the old paved asphalt like the wake of a boat. I could hear the lightning —even though I knew it was impossible. But the high-pitched whine of the buildup filled my ears.

I'd introduced myself twice to electricity. And today, it was determined to say hello back. I was going as fast as I could and used the lamppost to swing myself in the right direction, down the hill of my front yard.

The zap and blow of the electricity in the air pointing its finger at me sent me tumbling down the hill, my hair straight up like a human tumbleweed. Rain started then, my tears of relief mingling with it and getting diluted by it. I was okay. The lamppost was crooked and sparking. I was close to my front door— telling myself I was fine. I stood up and opened the door. It wasn't locked during the day.

Maybe I was imagining the connection between electricity and me. As I headed upstairs, another bolt came right through the sidelights by the front door and rang the old phone on the wall. And then I knew it was announcing itself fully in my life. And I could run, but it would still find me in my house.

My New Year's Day consisted of pigs in a blanket for breakfast and lunch. That's normal. I didn't have a weird compulsion for appetizer foods. It just made sense on New Year's Day because they were on sale at the store. And apparently, reminiscing about my past run-ins with death.

After Christmas with my parents, I was full up on holidays for a little while. It was nice that everyone had a cluster of birthdays in the summer, so I had a breather.

Mom had been pestering me about Poncy. And Poncy had been pretty aloof the whole time. I thought I caught him checking out Teva's ass, which was stupid because her man was not the forgiving type.

His gift to me was iTunes gift cards. He was proud of the

thousand dollars he'd given me because the total was written on the outside of the envelope in a black Sharpie marker.

The thing was, I couldn't imagine what the heck I could buy with that much money on iTunes. Mom was impressed. She took our picture and wanted the envelope facing out. I was tickled to see she'd set Poncy and me as her iPhone's wallpaper. It felt good to make her happy.

But I wasn't going back so soon after leaving. Poncy sent me a Happy New Year's email, and I'd responded with the same. But today was just for me, my pigs and my art. I had a whole section in the hallway that was still blank. And a blank canvas always got me worked up.

I laid out a drop cloth and mixed the paint to get the right base. Flesh colored. I put my music on loud because I liked to feel immersed when I created. I began. First—his hazel eyes. Had to get them right. When I felt like they were windows to the soul, I went on to the other features.

I had to remind myself to stop to pee. When I came back to the hallway, I stood a few feet away to see my progress and figure out what I was doing next spatially.

I tilted my head when I realized I recognized the person I was painting. It happened. My mind's eye would hold onto something and the creative side would sneak it into my art. I was shaking my head, wondering how obvious the resemblance would be when there was a knock on my front door.

"Maintenance!"

Oh no. We had three rounds of knocks and yells before they would come right in. I ran for my bedroom and grabbed a sweatshirt to put over my head. Had to hide the nips. That was rule number one. I made it to my doorway in time to see Bear and Paul, the maintenance man, letting themselves into my place.

I tried to block the painting. My style was a little abstract, but

I was pretty sure he would recognize himself. Sure enough, his gaze lifted from me to just past my left shoulder. I could tell from how high his eyebrows creeped up his face that he sure as hell did know what I'd done. He looked from me to the painting to Paul.

Paul had the look of a hungry man and he had his eyes pinned on the plate of pigs in a blanket.

"Have my wieners!" I did jazz hands.

Bear stepped in between Paul and me and pointed his fingers at the plate. "Oh hell yeah. I'm going to eat the hell out of those."

Paul seemed encouraged that Bear was willing to eat them, too, and asked if I had mustard.

"Sure thing. In the fridge. In the back. And if that one's empty, then there's a jar in the back of the pantry." I waved Paul toward the kitchen, but, of course, he knew the way.

Bear stepped up to me. "What is that?" He used the same finger he'd pointed at my pigs with to indicate the start of the portrait of his face.

"I paint people who catch my eye. Look around." I watched as he rotated his whole body to take a closer look. "That's my sister's husband. That's the lady that lived down the street when I was a kid. It's just a me thing." I shrugged my shoulders and lifted my hands as if I were carrying two plates.

Bear cursed under his breath. Paul hollered from the kitchen, "Not in the fridge!"

I yelled back but kept my gaze on Bear, "Then it's definitely in the pantry!"

"You don't have any mustard, do you?" Bear's whisper was rough.

I shook my head. I hated mustard but wanted to buy myself time to deal with this situation.

Bear raked his hands through his hair and then ran them back through to drag down the front of his face. "I'm not allowed to be involved with residents. At all. And that makes us look involved."

Before I could answer, he was in motion, peeking around the corner. He took off into my bathroom and ripped down my shower curtain and the suspension rod that held it up.

I whispered back, "That's my curtain!"

He ignored me and shouldered past, slamming the rod open to its widest setting. Using his superior height, he jammed it in as close to the ceiling as possible and then spread the curtain.

Paul came out of the kitchen, hitching his thumb over his shoulder. "I can't find it. Are you sure you have some? Hey, was that curtain there before?"

Bear and I responded together like we'd practiced it, "Yes."

"Oh. Could've sworn it wasn't. You know what? I have some mustard packets down in the office. I'll be right back. You're kind enough to give us the pigs, I can provide the condiments."

Paul had a huge smile that made me wonder if my obscene amount of wieners would be enough.

He closed the door behind him.

"Where's the office?" Bear had his arms folded in front of his chest.

"Across the complex. Does he have the golf cart?" I tried to get past Bear to see if his quick curtain trick had messed up my wet paint.

He put both hands up. "Wait. What are you doing? We can't do anything. Please don't throw yourself at me."

That stopped me in my tracks. "What? I'm checking to see if my art is okay. And see if my shower curtain is ruined. That paint is wet. But I'm not wet there, ladies' man." I pointed at my crotch. "Just because I painted your picture and you caught me with Veiny doesn't mean I'm pining for you." I heard it as it came out of my mouth so I had to concede, "Though I can kind of see where you're getting that idea now that I say it all out loud."

"Who's Veiny?" His eyebrows pulled together.

"My vibrator. He has a name." I was sounding crazier by the moment. At least my toy wasn't named Bear. Yet. It would make a decent middle name though.

"Do all girls do that? Name their sex toys?" He shifted his weight from one foot to the other.

"I don't know. We don't talk about that kind of stuff. Let me by." I pushed at his ridiculously hard chest. He took a big step back.

I peeked under the curtain. Everything was fine.

"Satisfied?" He spoke behind me. Close behind me. "I'm not an animal. I wouldn't wreck it."

Now it was my turn for a surprise. I underestimated the amount of time Paul would take to get his mustard and get back. He had a fistful of yellow packets and a pair of hungry eyes. I threaded my way through the two men to get some plates and napkins.

Bear was watching me like he couldn't trust the next thing out of my mouth, but I spent my time asking Paul about his holidays and he asked me how I was getting on with the new place.

Bear opened the scary box of evil, aka the fuse box, and was plucking around in there with obvious confidence. It made me doubt he'd even been recently shocked because he displayed no fear at all. A few times our gaze caught and I felt sparks in places that had no electrical wiring at all. I had to cross my arms over my chest when my nipples started peaking.

I watched his eyes move from my face to my chest and back up. When he returned to his task, his dimples showed up in his cheeks, betraying a smile I bet he was hoping to hide.

After Paul finished his snack, he thanked me and gathered his plate, taking it to the kitchen. In the silence Bear stopped what he was doing to point at the curtain covering the painting, mouthing, "You have to get rid of this."

What Bear didn't know was how stubborn I was. I hated to be told what to do when it came to my art. If I was doing a commission, things were different. But my art, my walls, my rules.

"No way," I mouthed back. I showed him with my hands that I meant business. He looked at my chest again and I crossed my arms. He made the got-caught-looking-at-the-tits face.

He towered over me, switching to a whisper, "You have to. I could lose this contract if they see a picture of me on your walls. Are you even allowed to paint them?"

"Yes. The owners appreciate art. And inspiration. Though I may have to make the wall version of you much angrier."

He ran his hands through his hair again, causing it to stick up. His sleeve fell a little and I saw the makings of a tattoo. I grabbed his hand and twisted it. It was a chain tattoo, the links disappearing under his sleeve. I held his hand steady and plucked the snap open. With more of his wrist revealed, I ran a fingertip over the image that wrapped itself around his muscled, strong forearm. I heard him whisper a curse.

"How far does this go?"

"You can't ask me that."

"It's gorgeous." I tried to pull his sleeve up farther.

Paul's cough made us both take a step back. "Hey, I'm going to head to the next few units to tell them we're coming. Don't want to catch anyone in their skivvies, you know."

I waved Paul off and Bear started packing up his tools in his box.

"We need to talk about this. But not here." He looked over his shoulder. "Can I get your number?"

I considered him. This was a way to see more of his tattoo. "On the condition that I get to see what you've got under there." I pointed to his entire chest area. If he had ink on his wrist, he probably had it everywhere.

"Fine. Whatever." Bear pulled a pen out of his pocket and

shoved a blank receipt from the little book he had in the side pocket of his tool bag my way.

I jotted my number down. "You better not be a murderer. Because I'll tell my family to look at that if someone kills me."

He took the paper and slipped it into the pocket below the name Harry that was embroidered there.

CHAPTER 6

BEAR

*W*ell, that was unexpected. Monday had straight-up painted my portrait on her wall. Now, it was actually pretty damn good. She had her own voice with her art. A stamp that was uniquely hers. But it was my giant mug on her wall, and it needed to come down. At least she didn't have Veiny glued to the wall.

And she and bras were not friends. I'd seen more of her nipples than I had of my own in the last week. Granted, she had clothes on, but it was hard to miss it when her headlights were on. As soon as I got done with the inspection on all thirty-two apartments, I texted the number she gave me.

Hey, it's Bear. Can we meet up at Meme's Bar? Tomorrow?

I waited a few minutes, looking at the colorful door from my driver's seat.

She answered quickly. **Sure, what time? And meeting up at a bar will go a long way toward helping people realize we are not involved.** She added a bunch of emojis winking.

She was right. Hopefully Meme's would let me rent out the little yurt they had installed in the back for private parties. I'd run the power to it and the owner had told me to stop by one night to impress a lady. This seemed to qualify.

I WAS WAITING in the yurt. I checked the heat to make sure the HVAC guy was able to work with the setup I had installed. It was a toasty seventy degrees, so everything was going great.

I was analyzing the outlets when she walked in.

The two times I'd met Monday, she'd been surprised. She hadn't had time to get ready. She was a complete knockout both times as well. The kind of girl whose pretty held up in any light. She was dressed for going out tonight and she smiled at me when I turned from the outlet to face her. I could see the teasing in the sparkle of her eyes before she offered, "Never off the job, huh?"

I walked close to her and took her jacket from her hands, having missed the opportunity to help her out of it.

Shoulders.

I was caught staring at her two creamy shoulders. She was wearing a soft lavender sweater that was pulled off both of her shoulders.

There were touches of jewelry. In her ears, at her throat, threaded in a braid in her hair. Her jeans were skintight and faded in spots, and she was wearing heeled boots that cradled her calves. I couldn't take my eyes off of her as I hung her coat on the rack by the yurt door.

Her jeans had little doodles all over them. Well, actually, they were in really strategic places. Places that enhanced the curves of her thighs and the flare of her hips.

And her damn face. Artists are usually good at makeup. I mean, in her case clearly. Defining her eyes was where she'd spent her time before coming tonight.

"You look like a masterpiece." I walked to one of the tables and slid out a chair for her.

She rubbed her arms and her heels tapped on the wood floor. She took the seat and helped me put it under her.

I was nervous. Like legit nervous to be around her. Maybe because the other two times I had been working and I had to stay calm when I was working with electricity. But Monday was comfortable when she went out to dinner.

"This is really pretty. I mean, the interior of the bar is a little disarming with all the skulls, but this, it's quaint. Like a tent, but sturdier. I like the hole in the roof. You can see the moon through it."

I watched her explore the space visually. The fairy lights made her smile. I looked at her, which then led to a small blush in her cheeks.

"Yeah. When they told me they were building a yurt out here, I thought they were a little crazy. But once I saw it had full size doors and windows, I figured it could work."

She put her brown eyes on me. So inviting. I'd only dated one girl, from middle school up until six months ago. Ella had blue eyes. I was used to watching her emotions change. But Monday had mystery in hers.

"Yurt sounds like something a cat would cough up." She picked up her menu.

I cringed. She was sort of right. Not very romantic—but this wasn't a date. It was a place where we could meet and not be caught. Where I could plead my case for painting over the giant mural of me in her apartment. Well, if she finished it. She seemed like a finisher. And then I had issues in my pants. Thinking of the gorgeous girl painting my face in her apartment. Granted the place was full of faces, but still.

She lifted her eyebrow. "Thinking about the mural in my place?"

Maybe my eyes were far easier to read than hers. "Yes, actually. I just wanted to tell you about the contract we have with your apartment building."

The yurt door flung open. A Meme's waiter plastered a wide smile on his face the second he saw Monday. Jealousy burned in my fists, which was unreasonable and viciously quick.

"Hi, I'm Pete. Can I get your drink orders?"

He spent far too much time staring at Monday's shoulders than I would have liked. I ordered a beer and Monday ordered a glass of sweet wine.

After he left, with one more peek over his shoulder at hers, Monday pushed her menu to the side and leaned forward. "Go on. You were about to tell me how you wanted to censor my artistic licenses in my own home?"

I let my head roll on my neck. She wasn't going to make it easy. The flighty girl that wanted to bury a burnt chipmunk with a spatula also had to be a ballbuster about legalities.

"It's my face. Do I have any rights as to how it's displayed?" I leaned forward as well.

She bit the tip of her tongue while she thought. "I'll answer after you take off your jacket."

It took me a second to remember she wanted to see my ink. "Fine. See how reasonable I am?"

I stood and slipped my leather jacket off, moving to put it on the hook next to hers. Her chair scraped along the floor as she stood. I wore a dark blue t-shirt on purpose so she could see the ink on my arms.

Her hands ran up my forearm, and I turned toward her, goosebumps forming on my skin where she touched me. "Oh wow. It's amazing. And chains. This is a gorgeous pattern. I love it. Super flattering to your muscles and veins and stuff."

She was disarmingly close to me. Absorbed in the art on my

body. Lost in her own curiosity. She pushed the sleeve up higher and coasted her palm over my shoulder, pushing the fabric toward my chest. I grabbed her hand and stilled it.

She gasped at the movement, and then looked into my eyes. I watched as she realized how intimate she had been—so quickly. "At least let me buy you a drink before you find out what color my nipples are."

Monday let her jaw drop and then pulled her hands away. "I'm sorry. I'm forward when I'm curious."

I looked from her lips to her eyes and back again, hoping it was clear that it wasn't really a problem.

The door flung open again, and I reacted before I could plan on it, catching the door millimeters before it slammed into Monday's head.

Pete apologized as he steadied the glasses on his tray. "So sorry. Shit. You guys are right here."

Monday had to step closer to me so Pete could get through the door. I didn't take my gaze off of her face. She saw my intense scrutiny and I watched her mouth. "Oh."

I could be wrong about a lot of things in life, but I'd bet an entire fortune on the fact that Monday was turned on by me right this second.

Pete placed our drinks down onto the table with cocktail napkins. Monday turned, her long hair tickling my arm.

Pete waited for us while we went back to our chairs. I wasn't able to hold hers out for her again, because Pete was in the way and took over the job.

She thanked him and took a nice sized gulp of her wine when she sat. She looked everywhere except my face while Pete went on about the appetizers they had on hand tonight. After she turned him down for a snack, I did the same.

"So, the boss told me you guys have the yurt for the entire night. Are you relatives?"

There was a little too much hope in Pete's question. I shot

him down. "No. We actually have to have a pretty important conversation."

I let the silence hang in the air instead of offering more information. Pete took the hint and saw himself out, telling us to signal him if we needed anything else with the computer on the wall.

I knew all about the computer because I was the one who programmed it. I nodded with a smile, and he finally left us alone.

I went back to my initial line of questioning. "My face?"

She hummed, "Mmm-hmm," while she looked at me.

Now, I had plenty of attention from the ladies, but I was so used to turning it down because I was taken. My heart was taken and locked down. The way I became an adult was different from other people. Ella was my soul mate. My person. The other half of my forever. There wasn't a person in either of our families that thought otherwise. By the time we were sophomores in high school, the conversations between my parents and hers were when, not if, we'd get married. Ella was a given. She was my identity.

And now, for horrible reasons, she wasn't anymore. And I wasn't open to another person—but Monday. Well, she'd gotten things started for me that I didn't think would ever happen again. I was attracted to her, and she was nothing like Ella.

"My face is on your wall, and in our contract with your apartment complex, we're not allowed to be, well, involved with any of the residents." I set my hands on the table.

"I'm not sure I understand. Don't you have to be involved with people to work in their apartments?" She tucked her hair behind her ear, revealing the three hoops at the top of her ear's shell.

I was going to have to spell it out for her. "Sexually..."

I watched as understanding hit her and then watched her nostrils flare as that understanding budded into anger. "Oh. So an artist can't paint a picture of a man without banging him? It's immediately assumed that I was so moved by your penis that I had to commemorate the moment by immortalizing you on my wall?" She took another large gulp of her wine. "Explain to me how that works because I'm pretty sure male painters have worked on nudes of women that they never slept with. But that's okay, because women are meant to be decoration, and our bodies can be viewed under the guise of art and no one ever questions a male painter, do they?"

Oh shit. I triggered something deep in her that had far more implications than I anticipated. Maybe I wasn't the only one in the yurt that had brought a bundle of unseen baggage.

"That's not what I meant."

Man, furious, she was on fire. She was intimidatingly worked up. And hotter, goddammit.

Her mouth needed a kiss to silence it, which I realized would be proving her point possibly, so I stayed rooted to my chair.

"Just because I paint you doesn't mean I've taken rides on your sexual bratwurst. Sweet fucks out loud. Men." She stood up and grabbed her purse, reaching inside to toss a ten-dollar bill onto the table. She put both of her hands on the table, and I begged myself not to peek down her sweater that gaped open as the ultimate challenge. "I'm going to paint the most realistic naked picture of you the world has ever seen. How about you stuff that into your outlet and smoke it?"

With that, she huffed out the door, the whole yurt shaking as she slammed the door.

This had not gone well. Not at all. And I couldn't chase her because I was hard as a rock. I drank my beer and then finished her wine. It took a half hour before I could pay my bill and take my blue balls home. I had a crush on her, and she hated me.

MONDAY

I stroked the finishing touches on the tip of Bear's penis. It was pretty much a third leg. I did my best to recreate his arm tats, but I had to use my imagination on his chest and legs. I decided on a clown and joker motif. His left leg and fairly large left nut were dedicated to the Joker from *Suicide Squad*. His right leg and right nut were a homage to the clown from the movie/book *IT*. His stomach had a really nice six-pack decorated with the words "I screw Monday on every day ending with a Y".

I was contemplating adding a nude of myself bending over on the corresponding wall, but realized I'd be shooting my side of the argument in the foot by doing the thing that I had screamed about.

Once I was happy with the shading and the hands (they were always the hardest. Well, in my mural Bear's dick was the hardest, and flatteringly large), it was picture time.

I went into my lingerie drawer and found the most scandalous piece. The lace teddy with the two boob holes and the thong with the bow at the top of my butt crack seemed like the most obvious choice. I hadn't worn it yet and wasn't sure I had the confidence to pull it out in the bedroom. The set had been fairly pricey, and there were no returns on things that you used to floss your butt with, so it was still in my drawer. Now, angry, I was ready to wield the teddy's power.

I put it on, with thigh highs and sky-high heels. I set up my phone to take a few minutes of burst pictures. I posed seductively and then outright explicitly in front of the nude picture I'd painted of Bear. The first was me covering my nipples with my forearms and giving him middle fingers. The second was me bending over, ass toward the camera, peering between my legs, and the last shot was me pretending to lick the giant dick that had *censored* painted on the underside. I changed out of my sex clothes and settled on the couch to see my work in the pictures.

After editing my favorite three, I sent the images to Bear with the middle finger emoji in every color it came in.

Then my mom called. I felt dirty swiping the sexy pictures up to answer her call. She was breathless, which was concerning. When Mom was excited, it meant bad things. Sure enough, she started talking about Poncy, almost out of the blue entirely. I had to work to find out the reason she was calling. She got around to mentioning my yearly donation of a painting session at the Hartford Greens Gala Auction.

I knew what it meant. Making nice with lots of my parents' super rich friends and trying to remember everyone's names. And the worst part was half of the ladies would look different thanks to their recent plastic surgery. Of course, when Mom reminded me that painting sessions went for far more if the artist was attending the ball, or if they were dead, I decided the best option was attending. She became breathless again. It was the way she got when my sister was getting married. She reminded me of the stepmother in *Cinderella* when she thought the prince was coming to visit.

And then she whispered that Poncy was coming down for a surprise visit.

"What do you mean a visit?" I felt alarmed thinking of Poncy showing up unannounced.

"Well, he did give you a thousand-dollar gift card."

My tongue froze in my mouth. Was my mother insinuating that Poncy had "bought" some time with me? I felt sensation come back as my cheeks heated up.

"To the Apple store. Mom, we've gone on a few dates. I don't think I'm ready for a weekend." I began pacing back and forth.

"This man is a Nutwell. If he wants to speed up the relation-ship, then you speed up the relationship. The more time he spends with you, the quicker the wedding comes along." I heard her sigh.

That was how she saw this. A way to be related to a Nutwell. She wouldn't care if I was happy or not.

The false sense of happiness I felt when she was delighted about Poncy deflated in my chest. I was a means to an end for Mom. I knew that Poncy and I were done. Sending suggestive pictures to Bear was not the actions of a woman that was eager to have a relationship with an affluent friend of the family.

I pulled back my living room curtains, spying Poncy's Mercedes parked in the handicapped spot. He was affixing his grandmother's handicapped placard to the rearview mirror.

For Poncy, the handicapped placard was his "VIP parking anywhere pass". It was super embarrassing to crawl out of his expensive car and watch people shoot dirty looks at us. But Poncy ignored it all, saying the peasants were just jealous.

My mother had laughed at that joke. I hadn't.

I spun and faced my pornographic picture of Bear. My revenge painting. Poncy would expect to be let into my apartment.

I had maybe ten minutes to cover it while Poncy searched for the elevator to get up to the second floor that didn't exist. I eyed my shower curtain again. Bear had used it before, and it had fit perfectly to cover the mural.

I leaped into action. I pulled down the rod and dragged over a chair from my desk, hopping up to cover the painting.

Honestly, this picture of Bear was a lot of damn work. But before I defiled it with a giant throbbing dick, it had been a really nice depiction of his strong jaw and clear eyes.

I dragged my chair back and then ran to the bathroom. It was odd to have the curtain in the hall, but worse was that I had no makeup on. Poncy hated when I wasn't all dolled up. He told me I looked like the help when I didn't have lipstick on. I tried to put on a hasty coat of mascara. It was too late for lipstick. He was already knocking on the door.

I ran to the door.

After I swung it open, he gave me a half-hearted, "Surprise!"

Poncy was handsome, no one could take that away from him. He was tall, blond, and wearing clothes that seemed to convey power. His watches were big, his nose was slightly lifted in the air, and his smile was chemically neon white. Like a Ken doll if he came from old family money.

"Monday Blue, how many times have I told you to dress like I might be here any minute? I swear to Christ, if I come home from work when we have kids, I better not see sweatpants and sandwiches."

"Hi, Poncy, it's great to see you, too." I went to my toes to offer him a kiss.

He put up his whole hand to block me. "I don't kiss bare lips."

I put my heels back on the floor. Poncy always had a correction. I never got it right out of the gate.

"What brings you down here?" I stepped back and let him in. He walked in like it was the enclosure in a poorly funded zoo.

"Oh, baby. I feel like I'm allergic to all of these materials." He picked up one of my pencils and used the eraser to move my living room curtain to the side.

"I'm sorry. The closest store is Target, so I went there and I think they're cute." Defensive. This was my first apartment on my own.

"Babe, I have a headache. My bag is down in the car. Can you go grab it? I'm going to catch a nap." And then Poncy went into my room and crawled on top of my bed with his pricy shoes on.

I sighed out loud, and then marched out the door.

CHAPTER 7

BEAR

I'd pissed Monday off. Clearly, she had some aggression as she finished up the painting of me. But the actual pictures she sent? Oh shit. I knew it was a clear *fuck you*. But hot damn. Monday in a teddy was about to light my brain on fire.

Was this sexting? Anti-sexting? I didn't freaking know. But it was amazing. And horrible. Because instead of a tasteful portrait of me, there was now an extremely pornographic life-sized picture of me in her hallway.

It had only been one day since our meeting at Meme's, and now I was headed back over to the complex. Mom informed me that the complex owner, Mr. Winfred, had requested me to check and replace some of the knob and tube wiring I'd pointed out during my last inspection.

It was another cash flow revenue for my parents. I had to do it. So I went to Monday's place. I figured I could ask one more time for her to alter her painting. Maybe finally get around to telling her my father's story. Explain why this contract was not just important to asshole me, but to my dad who had never done anything wrong to Monday Blue a day in his life. And ask her forgiveness.

I parked my truck, noticing a Mercedes in the handicapped spot. I'd not seen anyone parked in the special spots before, so I wondered if the complex had a new resident.

And then I watched as Monday trotted into view. Leggings and a t-shirt with a cat on it never looked better. Her hair was pinned up in a bun with two paintbrushes stuck in it.

Charming. She was charming again. What would it be like to walk into a house and have her puttering around for me? I tried not to let the image of her touching up the coloration of my giant painted penis flash through my head. And I failed.

She opened the door of the Mercedes and bent over, reaching inside.

Oh God. Leggings. Leggings literally used my balls as a punching bag. I shifted in my seat. She straightened up and went to the popped trunk. I watched as she took two suitcases and a carry-on out of the back.

They were obviously heavy and the gentleman side of me couldn't just sit there and watch her. I hustled out of my truck.

"Monday! Can I give you a hand?"

She whirled, one of the big suitcases toppling over. "Shit." I helped her right it as soon as I got within arm's reach.

Monday worried over the suitcase. "Is it scratched or anything? These bags are expensive."

I looked and saw a scrape on the corner. I pointed it out.

Monday was worried.

"Want me to see if I can buff it out?"

She wheeled it over to the back of my truck. I found my finest grade sandpaper and got down low, lightly touching it up until it blended in.

"Here you go. Almost like new."

44

She was chewing her bottom lip like the now barely visible mark on the bag would be a huge problem.

"You okay?"

Before she could answer, before I could talk to her about the porno-style pictures she'd sent me, a man called her name. Her colorful door was open behind him.

"Monday! Where's my bag? I need my headache medicine." He scanned the parking lot until he found her next to me. "Come on up already."

I crossed my arms over my chest and glowered at him.

"I've got to go." She dragged the bag back to the others.

I came behind her and picked up the two heavy bags, letting her take the tote. "I've got these."

She hurried up the stairs, and I was rewarded with the view as I carried the bags.

The guy pursed his lips at Monday like she was a misbehaving child. I set the bags in the doorway as Monday pushed past and brought the tote in.

He pulled out his wallet and fished out a one-dollar bill. He held it out to me while speaking over his shoulder, "A few of my suits will need to be taken out and possibly steamed. Where do you want to go out to eat? Is there anywhere around here that even has table linens?"

He was holding the dollar out to me. I kept my face set in an inquisitive but hopefully non-judgmental expression.

Monday came back, pulling one of the suitcases into the room. I lifted the other, ignoring the tip the guy was trying to give me. I saw that my painting was now covered up again with the shower curtain.

I heard the guy huff and watched out of my peripheral vision as he made a big show about putting the money away.

Monday touched the man's arm. "Let me make sure I got all the information I needed from him. Maybe get started on finding your meds?"

And then she ushered me out the door and closed it behind her. "Sorry. Thank you for helping with the bags and fixing the scratch, too."

I looked down at her, not giving her enough space. My dick was in charge and he felt like he'd gotten an invitation via text earlier.

"Who's that?" I was expecting a lot of different answers, but not the one I heard.

"My boyfriend." Her eyebrows worried closer together.

"Is he now?" I couldn't do the math of it. I had seen the hottest pics of her. She had a picture of my giant dick on her wall.

"Yeah."

"And he has a disability?" Now I was asking personal shit, but I was really disappointed.

"Oh no, he uses his grandma's placard so..." She let the sentence trail off.

I finished the sentence for her. "...he can be a five-alarm asshole?"

She reached behind her to double-check that the door was closed. "Don't worry about the mural. I'll paint over it if I get a chance."

"It's okay. It was pretty flattering." If she was going to bring it up, so was I. "You can send me pics like you took earlier anytime you want."

I felt slimy flirting with her knowing her assbag boyfriend was in the apartment but combined with the few things I actually knew about him, I felt like it might be a deserving situation. He made her carry his bags. He parked in handicapped spots for convenience.

"Listen, those were vengeful pics." She touched the doorknob again.

I lowered my voice. "I hope I piss you off more in the future then."

She looked from my lips to my eyes and back. "Can I ask you a question?"

"Mmhmm." I stepped closer.

"Do you think I'm kissable? Like, on the lips kissable?"

I could read between the lines.

"You should know that you are. All the time. Very kissable," I answered. She moved her hand from the doorknob to her mouth. "Can I show you?"

Her eyes widened, then she shot a look over her shoulder before meeting my gaze and nodding once.

I put my hands on either side of her face and she covered my hands with hers. I leaned down and kissed her gently and then deeper, running my thumb along her jawline. She backed up into the door and I pressed her against it. I didn't cop a feel, and I didn't press her with my dick. I just kissed her like she deserved to be kissed. She melted into me, for me.

And I took a step back. Her eyes were still closed, her lips still pursed. I heard a silent, disappointed noise leave her and noticed the goosebumps all over her arms.

"See?"

Her eyes flipped open and went wide. She touched her lips again.

I gave her the biggest smile I could and added, "There's more where that came from. Dump the assbag, then come see me."

CHAPTER 8

MONDAY

*W*ell shit. I watched Bear trot down the stairs, shooting me a knowing look over his shoulder once. So much for not being kissable without lipstick. I'd never kissed a man with lip piercings before. And it was very, very hot.

The door was pulled open behind me, and I almost fell against Poncy. "What the hell are you doing out here? If we are going for dinner, you need to get ready. You look like shit."

When I was growing up, the Nutwell name was part of our everyday life. The family had donated a lot of places in Midiville. We'd stop by the Nutwell car dealership when it was time for an upgrade. The county commissioners always had at least three board members with the last name Nutwell. We'd had a Senator Nutwell and even a Sir Nutwell, with a knighthood from the Queen and everything. In school, the Nutwells had donated the very most to every occasion, and always had two full page ads in any program that sold space.

The name carried weight, as my mother liked to say. Even when she said Nutwell, it seemed like the word dragged her lower lip down a bit.

So when the rumor mill was buzzing about Poncy Nutwell looking for a date from yours truly, it was like my mother was reborn. She put her laser focus on me and the way I was dressing and acting. The timing of it all had pissed her off. When finally one of her daughters had caught some Nutwell eye, I was moving out and into my own place three hours away.

Poncy and I have had two months to get to know each other. I was finding out that he was the human equivalent to a chicken breast without any seasoning.

And yes, I was guilty of basking in my mother's approval. But the dream of teaching art had too strong a pull on me. Mother had decided that Poncy and I would make it work, somehow. She believed in love.

Love was not what I had in mind when I thought of Poncy. By the time I had packed my things to move to Treasure, Maryland, I had an inkling that this wasn't going to work out.

Now, as I got ready in the bathroom for dinner, I heard Poncy grumbling around in my apartment.

He thought my working as an art teacher was a waste of time. According to him, I'd have time to fingerpaint with my own children down the line, so I didn't need to go so far to teach ones that I wasn't related to.

I thought of the sexy pictures I sent to Bear. I was wilder with him than I'd ever been before. Maybe because I was living on my own for the first time and being a bit rebellious.

I looked down at my outfit. A neat, tight, black cocktail dress, strappy heels and a bun with impeccable edges. My jewelry was tasteful, and I had a matching black jacket and purse.

When I came out of the bathroom, Poncy frowned. "Whose dress is that?"

He wanted to know the designer. "Michael Kors," I offered.

I wasn't sure, actually. Mom had purchased it for me, and I was pretty tactile, so I always cut out the tags, which was sacrilegious to her, who claimed eighty percent of the price was for the tag with the designer on it.

"I feel like it's so last season. Do you have anything more current?" He touched the sleeve like it was covered in six-day-old spaghetti sauce.

"Um, I haven't unpacked everything, so this is the best we can do and still get to the restaurant in time to be served."

Poncy rolled his eyes before declaring me fine. He grabbed his jacket from the closet and walked out the front door. I took a moment to get my jacket before I closed and locked the front door behind us. He was already in the car with it in reverse when I opened the passenger door.

He started rolling just as I got both feet in the car, leaving me to slam the door while moving.

I worked hard not to think about Bear. And the kiss. And all the chair holding and door opening. And the kiss. And those viper bite rings.

Poncy sat as if he was uncomfortable in his skin. He leaned one way, and then the other.

He poked at his pasta with his fork. "It's still not hot enough."

The server gave us a tight smile as Poncy snapped in his direction. If I had been closer to Poncy's hand, I would have pushed it down.

"Sir, you want us to heat it again?" The server put his hands behind his back.

"No, of course not. That will overcook the pasta. You'll have to have them make it from scratch."

I watched as the server's jaw twitched. "Of course."

"Maybe try eating it right away this time."

He'd refused to put his phone down when the last plate had been delivered with steam coming off of it.

He flicked his gaze to mine. "Their job is to make me happy and satisfied, no matter what it takes."

I covered my mouth with my hand, keeping the words inside. I didn't want a scene, but this wasn't going to work. After working with my kids every day, the things that Poncy valued and the things I valued were very, very different.

While he ate his fresh plate of pasta, he told me how annoying it was to have to travel the distance he did to see me. Poncy Nutwell was a complainer. Possibly a serial one.

After we finished dinner—Poncy returned his dinner twice because it wasn't hot enough—

we got to my door and Poncy decided he was going to sue the building for not having an elevator.

"It's living like animals to have to get the heart rate up so much after eating." He panted.

"I think it's good to move after a big meal."

I didn't tell Poncy that I was done with dating him, and I really should have. Instead, he went to bed. Traveled three hours to spend time with me, then he went to bed. I had to deal with the fact I'd kissed another man on my doorstep. I felt like a traitor, but it also sent a zing to my lady parts. Bear was a wonderful kisser. The press of the hard metal he had in his lip against mine sparked my imagination. I kept thinking about the guilty smile he sent me over his shoulder.

I tiptoed into my bedroom. Snoring, Poncy was stretched out in the center of my bed. I wondered what scared me about breaking it off with him. Disappointing Mom, for sure. I could picture her railing at me if I broke it off with a Nutwell. She'd romanticized them for me almost my entire childhood.

I closed my door slowly. I pulled the extension rod and curtain down, revealing the portrait. It looked lewd now. Using my favorite talent to give Bear the business felt a little nauseating.

I kicked off my heels and set up my paints. Originally, I was going to cover the whole thing with white, letting the blank wall cover what I had started, but the longer I stared at the painting of Bear, the more a new image came into view.

It took me all night. Of course, I was in hyper focus mode. I painted over the pornographic parts and added my hopes for our kiss instead. And a bit of the guilt. I added the attraction between Bear and me. With the light trained on the wall, I was in my element, creating. I took my name off his stomach and gave him tasteful tattoos. Just before I lay down, just to rest my eyes, I realized it might have been the best thing I'd ever done.

I WOKE up to a toe poking me in the center of my back, flicking my vertebrae. Startled, I sat up, ramrod straight.

Poncy was scratching his male parts with one hand and pointing at the picture of Bear with the other. "That's good. Like really good."

I pushed myself up and propped against the wall. My black dress had paint smudges all over it. My hands had paint on them as well, though that was their usual state.

He was right. Whatever had spurred the painting on my wall, it was damn near perfect. Now granted, Bear was still naked, but his no-no stick was carefully covered, partly with his hand and partly with the piece of foliage that was now incorporated into my wall mural.

"You should recreate that for the charity ball. But with my face, of course." Poncy headed off to the kitchen.

Either he missed the resemblance to Bear or he was willfully ignoring it. I was guessing it was the first. Poncy had a habit of looking for his own reflection in shiny surfaces. A parking lot and an office building were minefields for his vanity.

I touched my lips, then I looked at my fingertips. The paint was still a bit tacky and I was probably wearing a touch of it as lipstick.

CHAPTER 9

BEAR

*W*ell, I kissed her. And that was against my man code. She had a boyfriend. We respected that shit. But he was a dick. Who the hell parks in the mobility limited spots when they don't need them?

And damn, that kiss was all my dick could think about. Monday's lips were satin and her surprised eyes plus aroused response were a game changer.

She was trouble with a capital T. As I walked around the rest of the apartment complex, checking for the likeliest problems and marking them, I was waiting to see his car leave. Hopeful to watch him storm out, angry. It didn't happen, though, and eventually, it got weird. I had to head home. And his car was still there.

So either she told him and he didn't care that I kissed her or she didn't tell him. I wasn't in the headspace to socialize with my parents right now, so I went to my studio for the first time since I took over for Dad at his business. Between helping Mom maintain the house and keeping Hanning Electric alive, I didn't have time to come back. The mail had built up to a pile on the other side of the door. I had to give the metal door more of a push. After gathering it up, I made my way to the industrial elevator while I perused my bills.

After I cranked open the gate when I hit the second floor, I realized the place always had a faint odor of sawdust when I was away for extended periods of time. I went to the thermostat and turned up the heat. I really didn't have time for this stop. I needed to check in and see how Mom was doing and if there had been any emergency calls.

But kissing Monday required something. I needed an outlet. And I only had one that would do. I shed my jacket and put the mail I'd gathered on the countertop.

My studio was also my home—one giant room save for the bathroom. I'd remodeled most of it myself. Dad helped here and there, but I took pride in making the top floor of what had once been a mannequin warehouse a place to be creative.

I pulled the protective tarp off my current piece. Even though it was covered, I still wet a rag with warm water from the sink. There was a sink in the kitchen and another one in the living room area. I needed to wash off in a hurry sometimes. That wasn't the only unconventional setup here either. I had tons of outlets and cords. Welding guns and helmets hung from hooks on the wall.

Rubbing the wood down with the damp rag was a bit like painting. It brought out the colors and reminded me of the palette I was working with. Moisture was healing to dry wood.

I was working on a table. Well, the top of the table—it could go any which way really. If I added legs, it would be a big table.

I worked slowly, feeling the stress roll off of me. I missed this. I used my carving tool to work a bit more, smoothing out the river in the center. The table was almost done when Mom called about Dad. It felt good finishing the table off now, knowing that everything turned out okay. That Dad was still with us.

I laid the charges carefully and adjusted the volts. Now was the good part. The magic part. I electrified the table, angling the charge in such a way that the electricity became alive, singeing a path along the wood. The branches inched out, satisfyingly zapping a path that was organic and unpredictable.

The art. I often felt like I was just the maintenance man and the electricity was the artist. It used my hands and knowledge to speak its mind.

When I was young, I developed a knack for this. Becoming electricity's outlet. I was comfortable around it. It was like a wild puma that lived happily in my house. For most people, electricity was a utility. A way to get their favorite things started. I respected it for that. But I also felt a kinship with the river of energy that it worked in. Experiments in the garage while my father indulged me. He taught me to be safe. He taught me the principles of electricity to respect. It always followed the rules. If someone got hurt, it was because of human fault. Making mistakes. Electricity always did what it was supposed to.

I found this way to express myself. The channels that electricity took to pass through in the wood became frozen forever, stalled in time.

This piece was exciting because I wanted to work with a new element. After the table was charged and set, I carved a new channel out and mixed some resin. I poured it carefully into the opening, hoping it would represent a clear bit of water. It needed probably thirty-six hours to cure. I stepped back and took a look. I had high hopes for this table. It was opening another whole layer of expression. Adding a new element was so inspiring I had to sit down after tidying up my workspace and jot down notes.

And then I thought of Monday again. The artist in me had a

giant crush on the artist in her. Her work had such a stamp of ethereal emotion. Even the bulging penis.

And she had a boyfriend. I exhaled and picked up my phone. Four messages from Banks, my roommate from college.

In town.

Need a drink.

You need a drink.

Make the drink in our faces.

Then a picture came through of two ice-cold looking IPAs sitting on coasters. Using the context clues, I was able to figure out that he was at 3 Bends, a bar attached to a restaurant downtown.

I responded. **Keep it cold. I'll be there in 15.**

Banks always had great timing, because sitting down and laughing with him for an evening was the best way to take my mind off of my homewrecking daydreams about Monday. I jumped into the shower and had myself in my truck wearing a white button-down shirt and a pair of my favorite jeans in under fifteen minutes.

3 Bends had valet parking, which sucked, but they also had the best selection of local brews, which made up for it.

I drove up to the valet and got out of my truck, smiling. "Thanks, dude." The valet returned the smile and handed me the valet ticket.

I recognized the voice behind me right away as I watched the valet pull away.

"I'm sorry. Ugh, my friend forgot to get the valet ticket."

It was Monday Blue. I spun on my heel, and I was basically looming over her, her back to me.

"Miss, do you have the license plate number? Make and model?"

She wrung her hands together and turned her head to look at the upstairs window. "I left my phone upstairs and I never notice stuff like that. I'm so sorry."

"Can your boyfriend come down and tell us?" The valet seemed perplexed.

"It's a Mercedes with a vanity plate BTR THN U," I said.

Monday turned slowly before looking up to my face.

"You."

She was going for a buttoned-up receptionist look. It was harsh. Her hair was pulled tight and her makeup was an expert level of shading.

"Me," I responded. I wanted it to come out as a wiseass, but instead, I sounded super grateful.

Her cheeks flushed as she looked me up and down. "Are you following me?"

I folded my arms so I wouldn't pull her in for another kiss. I would wipe all the lipstick off first, though. With both my thumbs. Then I would taste her mouth. Her anxiousness. All this pretend stuffiness.

"Not today. I'm meeting a friend for drinks." I tilted my head in the direction of 3 Bends.

Her mouth made a little O, but she said nothing.

"You and the guy here?"

She touched her hair like she forgot that it was pinned up. Her fingers fluttered before falling.

"Yes. I forgot to get the valet ticket, so I'm trying to remedy that." She spun back to the valet.

The valet already had the ticket in his hand from my description. She took it gratefully and then patted her dress for pockets. A tip. She wanted to give the guy a tip and I bet she left her purse up at the table, with her lazy ass boyfriend and her phone.

I dug into my pocket and coughed up a five. "Thanks, man," he told me.

"Oh. Thanks. I'll pay you back." She looked at me again. The up and down again. Hesitating at my forearms, flicking back to my lips, then my eyebrows. Checking out my piercings.

It sent a flicker of lust through my body. Shit.

"Why is the douchebag not doing this?" I motioned to the valet stand.

"Uh, Poncy? Um. Well, it's my job as the navigator..." her voice trailed off, possibly hearing how much bullshit was packed in those few words.

"Wow. Poncy. Never heard that one before. You cold? We should get you back inside." She shivered as if my suggestion made it true.

I walked over and held open the door to the restaurant. She touched my hand. "Thank you. I amended the picture last night. It's very tasteful. Just so you know."

"Oh good. Thanks. I appreciate that." I let my tongue peek out as I thought of what it would be like to kiss her again.

Banks yelled out from in front of me, "Wait up, Bear!"

I watched as Monday slipped through the open door. I wanted to follow her. Take her to her table and pull out her chair. Instead, I nodded at her like I was the official doorman and released the handle. I wasn't here for her, or with her.

Banks came down the stairs and slapped me on the back. "You old fucker. How the hell are you?"

I grabbed his hand and used it to pull him in for a half man-hug. Banks and I had gotten into a lot of trouble together in college. I had a feeling we would be recounting a few of those stories over tonight's pints.

"I'm great. No complaints. How are you? How is Merry?" I sidestepped so that our reunion would not be in the way of new patrons trying to get to their tables.

"She's fantastic. Busts my balls every day. Always has a honey-do list." Banks pulled out his phone and showed me his lock screen. Banks had met Merry two weeks before graduation. I'd never seen a man fall so fast or hard as when the redheaded bookish girl had taken Banks' hand.

"As it should be. Hell, should we take this upstairs? You

know once we get talking we're bound to not even take a breath." I pivoted toward the stairs.

"Oh yeah. I want to taste some hops on the back of my tongue while I look at your baby blues. And I have two waiting at our table. I've been keeping our table warm until I saw you through the window." Banks strode confidently into the restaurant and up the stairs. We've had drinks here on occasion since college, and it's always a favorite. Their sliders are epic.

When we got to the top of the stairs, Banks nodded at the host as we headed to the table. I scanned the room looking for her. I hadn't realized I was doing a spot check until I found her. Rage flooded my eyes and fists. I just hated Poncy on sight. He was talking loudly on his phone, his heavy, large watch pulling on his arm. I hoped some of his arm hairs would get caught in the links on the band. He deserved that.

Monday locked eyes with me and I let part of my smile pull up one side of my lips. She looked far too good to be ignored, but that was certainly what was happening.

Banks pulled on my shirtsleeve. "Bud, you let me know when you're done staring daggers at that couple and I'll send you a text about a hitman—if you need one."

I forced my gaze to Banks. "Nah, I'm not up to anything, I swear."

I followed Banks who led me out to the balcony. I checked again. I couldn't stop myself. Monday had whispered outside that she'd changed the portrait and I was surprised to feel a touch of regret. I liked the fighting version of Monday. The mad version. She was fun and scary.

"So, is that girl an ex or something?" Banks pointed to the table that had my attention as we sat down.

"Or something. Tell me about your job. How's the insurance world treating you?"

Banks started in on a story about a cow breaking into his neighbor's house and mounting the kitchen island like a prospective bovine lover. The neighbor had so many house alarms and cameras that the whole thing wound up going viral on the internet. Banks had the case. His co-workers were giving him the business by leaving milk and cheese on his desk. Because he was sort of famous after the homeowner made a video of Banks' very serious face taking notes on hump swings and hoof marks.

"Well, it's never a dull day." A round of apps arrived at our table. Monday was still surly looking. Poncy was still on the phone.

Not my place. Not my girl. Mind your business. Mind your manners.

The pep talk was working so far.

"So give me the update on your dad. I saw on social media that he was working on rehab." He leaned in and snatched a nacho.

"I forgot that Mom posts updates. I told her to keep that on the down-low so customers don't get nervous." I pulled out my phone and navigated to the social media app in question. Sure enough, Mom had asked for prayers, a ramp for the stairs, and a peanut butter cookie recipe.

"I wouldn't concern yourself with it. Everybody trusts the hell out of you. Shit, you're like having a Disney World's firework technician light a birthday candle. Overqualified." He took a swallow of his beer.

I shrugged. He was probably right. What I did with my art was insane. I had to understand the basics of electricity, do the math, take into account the wetness of the wood—all of it to make a table.

"I heard someone down at the hardware store talk about getting some new fancy LED yard lights and they mentioned your company. One of them even said now that you were on board, he was pretty sure Hanning would be even more tech forward." Banks scratched his neck.

It was nice to hear that I had a good reputation—well, at least for now. I looked back over at Monday. Until she revealed her naked picture of me, or it was found out, then my reputation would take a dive for sure.

She'd taken out her phone and was scrolling on it. The server was standing near their table, and I watched as something finally caught Poncy's attention. He was giving the server a very thorough once-over. Or twice-over.

Monday glanced up from her phone and her face changed as she observed Poncy staring at the server's ass like he was trying to use telekinesis on it.

She stuck her tongue in her cheek and shook her head. I could almost hear the last straw breaking in her head. She slammed her palms down onto the table and the silverware hit the glass.

She didn't yell, but I was also intently staring at her so I knew she had directed an "Enough" in Poncy's direction.

Monday gathered up her purse and tucked her phone into the front pocket as Poncy did his very best to look like an innocent angel. "I can't even look?" I heard him say.

Banks cleared his throat. "Hey, do you need to get involved over there in Angel Face's situation?"

I grimaced as I thought about it. I mean, if Poncy tried anything dodgy, clearly I was going to make sure he didn't touch Monday. But this was her boyfriend, who had come to visit. Sure, she and I kissed, but I had no idea how serious Monday had taken that.

She rested her palm on her forehead and took a deep breath before telling him, "That's it. Don't come back to my place. We're done."

Monday turned on her heel and headed for the door. Poncy tossed up his hands but stayed where he was, trying to catch the eye of any fellow diners. I dropped my gaze. It wasn't cool of me to be prying in Monday's life just because we were in the same restaurant and we'd kissed. Poncy snapped his fingers at the server and then downed the rest of his drink. "I need a refill. Now."

I watched as the server pasted a no teeth smile on her face. No one liked being treated like a servant. Many occasions people referred to me as the help while I was working on their electricity and the tone went right through me.

"Let me just make sure that she has a ride home." I pushed away from the table.

"Good, man." Banks nodded at me.

I got to the front windows in time to see Monday sliding into the back of a vehicle. She had called a ride service. She would get home. Poncy was still here. I liked that I could keep an eye on him while Banks and I caught up with each other.

I loved that Banks worked through my distraction because he knew I was preoccupied. We'd known each other for far too many years. He knew I had my heart somewhere else.

CHAPTER 10

MONDAY

I was sitting on the floor, looking at the painting of Bear on my wall. I'd locked my front door. I was done with Poncy. Enough was enough. I was facing some real hard truths tonight. I was going to have to tell my mother that her dreams of a Nutwell wedding were very far off base, and it wouldn't be easy.

I had real joy here in Midiville. I was staring at this painting and thinking about going back to school after the break. I had a student that was in a wheelchair and had a lot of difficulty communicating. His special education teacher had worked wonders with communication buttons and his adaptive iPad that was really letting us have insight on his personality. Leo's excitement had been getting more and more apparent in art class. And I didn't know why but looking at this painting gave me an idea. An electric idea. I'd love to make a painting and have Leo's adaptive buttons painted on a large scale. A huge scale. A mural.

The satisfaction of painting things on walls felt powerful. It was like shouting. And Leo might never be able to actually shout, but for a while it'd feel like he was. I loved it.

I loved the idea and was instantly excited to think about the logistics of making it happen. I could design a whole lesson for the kids that emphasized memorializing their ideas, their opinions, or even just their likes.

I'd need a co-collaborator, of course. I'd have to be wired. Electricity. I snorted. Bear would be perfect. I wondered how I could bring that up.

That gave me joy. Not thinking about a fussy wedding to a man that had eyes for everyone but me in the restaurant tonight. It wasn't that I was jealous, it was more that I realized I was wasting time. His and mine. Poncy wasn't what I needed or wanted in a partner. Maybe being on my own had cleared my vision. Mom's pressure that the Nutwells were a perfect match just wasn't that important when I was dreaming up ways to help Leo make his art.

Earlier, Bear had met my eyes every time I dared to look over in the restaurant. That rush was something else. He was... dreamy. I touched my lips, thinking of him. I wish I weren't letting my mother down so hard, but I knew now that it just wouldn't work.

At that exact moment, Poncy slapped on my apartment door hard. It'd started raining. I mean, it was the middle of the night. I had to let him in to sleep, right? Right?

BEAR

I was sitting in my work truck watching this dick potato slam on Monday's door. He'd drunk himself into a stupor while making snide remarks to the servers about how he was a man of means.

The valet wouldn't give him his car keys when he was finally ready to leave.

I timed my departure with his, and Banks slapped me on the back on our way out. "So let me know when you get married to the chick that left him, or if you need to bury his body. I've got time."

I stuck out my hand and we shook on it. We'd had a great night, and I appreciated his full support.

I followed Poncy's Uber back to Monday's apartment. And listen, I know that has a stalker flavor to it, but I had to be sure she was safe. Hanning men just don't leave a lady hanging out to dry. I felt like she was a little trapped in the situation. And a chick that would bury a roasted chipmunk with a spatula was different. Caring.

I wanted to pound on Poncy. Maybe I had a little aggressive rage left over from Dad's health incident. It's really hard when someone you love is in pain and their worst enemy is their body.

I got out of my truck and walked in the direction of her apartment. All bets were off now. I was going to make sure she was okay.

CHAPTER 11

MONDAY

*P*oncy's eyes were pointing in two different directions. It's what happened when he drank. He had a lazy eye that was mostly kept in line, but if he was tired or inebriated, he seemed to have difficulty straightening them out. It occurred to me that he'd been drinking to that point at every date we'd had so far. Well, that dinner had been our last.

"Listen, I don't understand why you have to be such a bitch. A man's gonna look. That's what a man's going to do. You better be used to it when you're dating me."

He was pointing at me, his finger inches from my nose.

"No." I slammed the door hard, and I heard him squeal on the other side. I was done making excuses for his behavior. I walked into my bedroom and dragged his suitcases through the apartment. I opened my sliding door and brought them out onto the porch. I lifted the smaller one first. I checked over the railing and saw that it was clear—no one would be injured after I chucked this luggage.

Then I picked up the second one. It was far bigger. Instead of pulling my lower back with the weight of it, I unzipped it and began pulling out clothes like a magician with a scarf in his sleeve. It was freeing. Expensive pants? Overboard. Polo shirts with the yacht club embroidered on it? Yeeted. Million-dollar electric toothbrush for his self-proclaimed movie star teeth? Heave-ho.

Then, when I'd lightened the load, I was able to tip the large suitcase into the yard. I was smiling. I wasn't angry anymore. This was great. Later. Goodbye. Never again.

Poncy joined me on the deck.

"What the hell?" I stepped back.

"What the hell? You tossed all my shit out there?" He gestured to the yard.

"I locked the door." I put another few feet between us, looking to get back into the apartment.

"Your mother gave me the key. Of course." He held up the offending piece of metal.

"Of course." That would be Mother's way of trying to encourage Poncy to spend more time with me. Literally an invitation to her daughter. I snatched the key from his hand. His reflexes were slowed by the drinking, so it wasn't hard to do.

"Give that back." He was pointing again. "And you're going to pick those up and take them to the dry cleaners tomorrow. That's expensive stuff."

Two more backward steps and I was able to get inside. As I started to close the patio door, Poncy grabbed the edge, preventing me from slamming it shut.

"Monday, stop this." He tilted his chin up and tried to stare me down. Only his left eye was cooperating.

Movement behind Poncy made me flinch. A tall, dark figure spun Poncy and coldcocked him right in the face.

I screamed as Poncy fell to the porch like a boneless porkchop. The man that was the puncher leapt off the porch like Spiderman.

I felt my jaw drop, but then had the wits about me to close the door totally and lock it. I was saved. And I was screwed. In that order.

BEAR

I'd landed in the yard after swinging down from Monday's balcony. My ski mask was in place and my hand was throbbing.

This was bad. Super bad. Not only did I have my naked portrait on the wall of this beautiful girl's apartment but I'd just assaulted her boyfriend. My hand hurt so much, I was actually a little afraid I might have killed him.

I staggered back in time to see Monday shut and lock the door. The silhouette of her douchebag boyfriend (well, hopefully ex-boyfriend judging from all the clothes that had fallen in front of my face moments before I had to act) was still visible through the slats in the deck. She was safe and I was not. I needed to get the hell out of here.

I tried my best to look like I belonged, and even stopped to investigate a wire before I got to my truck and started it up.

An ambulance's siren was in the distance. I shifted the old truck into drive. It might be time to address this whole thing with Mom and Dad because I may have just set all their plans up in flames.

Monday was safe, and that was all that mattered. I needed to head home. To my parents' house, actually. It was time to confess to Mom and maybe Dad how much of a problem I'd created here. But first, I just waited. I couldn't get myself to leave.

MONDAY

It was Bear that punched Poncy. I didn't register it until after I was inside the apartment, but that had been Bear's cologne that I'd smelled. My lady parts recognized it first, and then I did.

Poncy was flopping around on the porch. I had to call an ambulance for him because the sound of the punch told me it had to have done some damage.

He'd let himself into my place after I'd walked out at the restaurant. I wasn't sure if it warranted an assault, but I felt way better with the door between Poncy and me closed.

The police knocked on the door and I showed them out to the balcony. The female police officer was paying close attention to my story of an attacker jumping onto my porch like Spiderman and then leaving the exact same way.

"He just swung up here? All the way on the second story?" She was skeptical. I waited to see what Poncy would say, and he was telling even more of a fantastic tale than I was.

"There were three of them. And they were coming after my girl." Poncy's lip was swelling.

It certainly was just one person. One tall person that could climb anything. A fearless person. And one that I saw in the restaurant tonight while I was angry with Poncy.

"I'm not his girl. I tossed his stuff outside." I pointed to the balcony.

I saw the policewoman give her partner a knowing look. "A domestic."

And I guess that would be considered what this was, even though Poncy didn't live with me.

"I don't want him here. Can you make him leave?" I crossed my arms over my chest. It was much later than I expected to be awake.

"If he doesn't reside here, we sure can see him out. He's going to have to go to the hospital and get a few tests. He hit his head pretty hard judging from the bump." The male police officer used a flashlight to look over the porch while the EMTs maneuvered a gurney into my apartment.

"These steps are a bitch."

"So's my girlfriend." Poncy looked from one man to another, trying to get someone to agree with him.

I gave my statement while Poncy was strapped onto the rolling bed. He tried to get me to agree to see him, but I refused. Somber. It was a somber evening. The violence was unexpected, but this fork in the road of my romance with Poncy had been coming for some time. *Never date someone to make your mom happy.* That was my takeaway here.

Poncy started complaining on his way down the stairs about the bumpy ride. I bid good night to the police and closed and locked my door. It was going to be morning before I knew it, but I also needed to face the giant mess I'd made outside my downstairs neighbor's place. I was going to have to clean it up.

I grabbed two trash bags and my keys. Late night trash bagging felt like a really classy way to end my evening.

I took the tiny sidewalk around the building until I got to the pile of Poncy's belongings. I kicked them with my shoe. It was cold out and I was not about to be gentle with his crap.

"Hey." A soft alert.

I spun around. "Hey." It was Bear.

"You okay?" He stepped into the light so I could see him clearer.

71

"I'm fine. Poncy is on the way to the hospital." I bent at the waist and grabbed a fistful of expensive fabric.

"I'm glad he's alive." He stepped closer and gently lifted the other trash bag from my grasp. He started collecting the strewn belongings with me.

"Are you? Because you hit him damn hard." I straightened up just when he did the same.

Maybe it was because he worked with electricity and I was afraid of it, but I swear it felt like a crackle between us.

"I didn't like how he was treating you." He lifted one shoulder.

"Me neither, if I'm being honest." I grabbed one of Poncy's shoes.

"What are you going to do with this stuff?" He grabbed the matching shoe from the grass and held it out.

"There's a donation collection station on my way to school. I think his clothes would be great in there." I donated to it all the time.

Bear lightly bit his lip and lifted an eyebrow. "I like it. Force him to do some good."

"He needs some karma points, that's for sure." I grabbed the last of Poncy's things and Bear held out a hand so he could carry both bags for me.

"Let me." He tossed them both over his shoulder like he was Santa Claus.

"Thanks. For all that." I should have said more. *Thanks for the valet money, for hanging around to make sure I was safe, for helping me now.*

"Anytime. I know what you can do with a paintbrush, so I want to stay on your good side." He started around the building, and I went with him. "Should I be expecting the cops at my place?"

I shook my head. "They're looking for the three guys that Poncy believed he got the best of. So my guess is no."

"So you know it was me?"

I led him to my car and hit the trunk unlock button. "Yeah. Everything seems to be about you lately."

He put the bags into my trunk. "Is that a good thing?"

"I should probably say no. But yeah, it's a good thing." I swung my keys on my finger.

Making Bear smile was a wonderful bonus to the evening. His white teeth and cute dimples highlighted his sparkling eyes.

"You shouldn't be around that guy again. He's the kind of person that seems to escalate."

"I'm sensing that. I'll get a reprimand from my mom in the morning, speaking of escalation." I felt my stomach twist with the thought of it.

Her dreams of a Nutwell wedding were being flushed down the crapper. There was no way I could talk myself into a relationship with Poncy when I felt like this with Bear.

There was a full silence between us. I had things I wanted to say and even more things I wanted to feel, and all of them involved Bear. But Poncy and I had literally just broken up. I needed to put some time in there.

He nodded like he could read my mind. "You head up and I'll just make sure you get in your place safely."

It was the kind of cold crisp you only found in the dead of night. The stars had sharp edges that intensified against the deep night, but they had nothing on the way this man looked at me.

"Okay. I'll head up." I stepped backward a few times until I had to turn around. "Thanks again."

He crossed his arms in front of his chest. "Anytime."

I clicked my tongue. A tall, tattooed guy offering to punch out an asshole anytime was a great way to head up a set of stairs.

Swishing my hips a little extra was overboard, but I did it anyway.

Bear was still by his truck when I peeked over the railing. He nodded, reassuring me that he didn't take ensuring my safety lightly.

When I locked the door behind me, I was looking at my version of Bear on my wall. It needed work. I was missing his bravery, that flare in his eyes, and the way the veins in his forearms swam just under his tattoos.

I had to work on it again in the morning. Get it perfect.

CHAPTER 12

BEAR

I was done making breakfast for Mom and Dad when they finally came down to the table. Scrambled egg whites, turkey bacon, and thick slices of whole grain bread rounded out my offering.

Mom looked sleepy but soft when she smiled at me. Dad was shaky but determined. I held out his chair at the table. "Son."

I made sure he eased carefully into the cushion.

"Dad, all the way down the stairs today. Nice work." I headed over to the coffee pot.

"So, to what do we owe this special treatment?" Mom added cream to her cup after I gave her a pour.

"A guy can't visit his parents just to make them breakfast?" I added coffee to Dad's mug.

He wrapped his hands around the cup. "I'm sure it had nothing to do with the police presence at the apartments last night?"

"You already tuned in to the town gossip?" I should have

known better. Dad was basically an institution in town. Everyone knew him, and his longtime friend at the police station, Frank, never forgot to tell Dad anytime one of our clients or properties had activity.

My family? We were talkers. We talked all the time. Very few decisions were made without at least hearing their opinions. I mean, I was ready to take on the family business— clearly, I had been training my whole life.

As soon as I needed to, I stepped up. I took over. But things like the naked portrait and the scorched chipmunk would normally have been fodder for our conversations. They would give me good-natured ribbing and I would laugh.

Now every mistake went through a hyper microscope in my mind. How would it affect Dad? Could we keep things afloat if he needed more care? We'd gotten this first round of bills under control, but if he had a relapse we might be looking at a different future.

I didn't want to give Mom more stress. Her focus was on Dad's recovery, and that's right where we needed her.

But still, I wanted them to also know. Be aware that I was having this issue.

"I was sort of involved last night." I grimaced as I waited to see their reactions.

"How so? You had something to do with a girl having boy trouble that required a man to climb a porch, lay a meat sandwich right in his kisser, and then hop off said porch?" Dad took a slow sip of his coffee.

He was onto me. I looked at Mom. She tried to hide her grin in the curve of her coffee mug rim.

"You know?" I put my fingers behind my neck and tilted back in my chair.

"It just reminded me of you, is all." Dad set his cup down.

"I'm sorry. It was me. I did that, and now I'm scared it will affect the business."

Mom put her foot on the leg of my chair and tipped me forward so I wouldn't tilt anymore.

"Is she worth it?" Dad lifted his brow.

"Every girl is worth it." I tapped my fingers on the table, looking at the bruised knuckles.

Mom got out of her chair and hugged my head before kissing the top of it. "We raised you right."

After Mom was done making me her own personal cuddle toy, I laid it out for them. How Monday had painted the portrait, how we had sort of fought, meeting her in the restaurant, and then down to coldcocking Poncy last night.

All Mom had to offer was, "Monday is a unique name."

My father bobbed his head up and down. "That it is."

"Aren't we concerned? Like at least a little bit?" Now I was perplexed.

Dad shrugged and then winced. The motion must have pulled on his scar. "Life is a journey, my boy. We don't always know the why of something until we're well past it."

Mom looked equally serene.

"Are you both taking Dad's drugs? You are way too calm." I pulled my phone out of my pocket and checked my notifications. Two emails and no calls.

Mom chuckled. "With what we've been through? I think we just love the moments we get with each other and you."

I finished my coffee while the two of them made eyes at each other. The near-death experience had given them some sort of panic sedative. Which was good for them, but also left the concern on my shoulders. Because I knew how expensive it all was and I didn't want Dad to go without medical care at all. He needed to make choices based on the look he was currently sharing with my mother, not on his wallet.

After I hugged them both goodbye, I promised to keep them updated. Mom just wanted to meet Monday.

CHAPTER 13

MONDAY

I was sick of the it's-Monday-on-a-Monday joke, but nine times out of ten, someone launched it at me at the beginning of the work week.

My phone was off. I mean, I always had it on silent at school, but it was off off. I was anticipating that Mom would be blowing it up. She would FaceTime, then call, then text, then email in that order to give me a piece of her mind. I could avoid all the communication except for the email here at work. And yup, her email pinged through. The subject line was NUTWELL!! I skimmed right over that one.

I was going to help Leo today, and his class started in just a few minutes. I pulled the large iPad off its charger.

When the automatic door began to whine, I turned off all my head static. The fight with Poncy, the fight with Mom, my feelings for Bear. Instead, there was just the wide grin of Leo. Sandra, his aide, was pushing him. Behind her we had a few others in the class. Two were nonverbal as well, but art was their voice. They loved to create. They rushed to their seats to add to their pastel projects that they were in the process of finishing. Next up for those two would be clay. I knew they would love it.

I sat in front of Leo as Sandra locked his wheelchair. In my head my new idea had worked. I had the Smartboard on behind me. I used a picture of Leo's mom that he had in his file and created it into sectioned blocks of color.

I laid out the pre-marked buttons that had primary colors. After I told Leo what I was going for, I had no idea if it'd actually work. His eyes darted all around, but every once in a while they landed on my face. Just a knowing in the back of my mind hummed.

"Okay, let's start with Mom's hair." I tapped on the iPad and the shape was outlined on the Smartboard.

After I placed two buttons close to him, I pressed each one to show him how they worked. Brown and yellow were his two choices.

And then I waited, giving him the patience and permission to take his time. I stayed focused on him. I didn't want Leo to get overwhelmed. It was important for me to catch his choice right at the moment it occurred. He'd had difficulty with object permanence in the past, so I wanted the gratification of the choice to be as close to immediate as possible.

Leo started his process of moving his hand of his own volition. The connection from his choice to his actual movement was slow but deliberate.

He placed his hand on the brown button and didn't give up until he had depressed it enough to emit the sound, "Brown," that I had recorded earlier in the day.

Instantly, I hit the blocked-out portion of his mom's picture and the color turned brown.

His smile overtook him, forcing his head back a bit. Sandra led the other kids in a round of applause. Small wins were big wins here. I was flooded with pride as Leo and I painstakingly worked through his first portrait.

This was what I was here for. I knew it. My day was too busy to respond to my mother, and I was grateful for that.

BEAR

The apartments where Monday lived were presenting some new shorts in the system. I was halfway through the inspection that Mr. Winfred had requested following the New Year's pole fire. A previous electrician had really gone on the cheap when wiring this place.

The complex manager, Roy, stopped by on a golf cart so I flagged him over.

"You see these outlets? How they don't have a ground fault circuit interrupter switch? The last guy had looped all of these outlets into just one."

Roy scratched his head. "I thought this was all up to code?"

"It should be, but I'm going to have to replace any outlets that aren't GFCI enabled. And some of these outside outlets are really meant for indoor use. I think the little chipmunk that died on that pole had really helped us prevent a catastrophe." I'd fix the outlets on Monday's unit first, obviously.

"Can you work up the cost of the job? I mean, we have to do it. But I want to make sure Mr. Winfred knows what he's getting into." Roy threw the golf cart into reverse.

"It's going to take a bit of time. It's a big job, but I can get you a realistic projection of cost by Friday." I glance around the interior of the courtyard, surrounded by the buildings that were neighbors to Monday's building. There were a crapton of outlets. A big job. A costly job. If I got to continue with this project, it would set up Dad really nicely.

Despite their nonchalance about my confessions this morning, I knew I had to keep my employment here chaos free. No more punching people when spying on the beautiful girl in 3B.

I spotted a pair of men's underwear trapped in a tree under Monday's balcony. A great reminder of the focus here. I needed to focus on electricity. And just as I thought it, I was checking her apartment to see if I saw her moving around inside.

I was doomed.

CHAPTER 14

MONDAY

I should've expected my mother to be at my place. I mean, even if she was a concerned mother, not hearing back from your kid would be concerning. Not that she was worried about my physical welfare.

She was in front of my apartment wearing layered neutrals and a long, high ponytail. Her giant black sunglasses were low on the tip of her nose. She had disdain on her face as if she was standing in an unkempt pigsty as opposed to outside a pretty nice apartment.

"Mother." I had brought home my work computer and a few canvases to grade. She did not offer to hold anything as I juggled everything to get my apartment keys.

"Monday." The tone. If I could bottle that tone, it would work as a repellent. No one wanted to deal with this woman when she had that tone.

I cracked open the door and silently kicked myself for not

replacing the shower curtain in front of Bear's portrait after using it for my morning shower.

It wasn't nearly as lascivious as it had been, but it still had a nutsack, so the awkwardness was sure to be prominent in our conversation.

My mother followed me in and closed my colorful door. She was staring at the elephant in the room—or more specifically, the elephant's trunk.

I set my stuff down and poured myself a glass of wine. I waited in the kitchen for my mother to follow me, but eventually I had to go back to the living room.

"Is this what an art degree does for a person?" She waved a hand at Bear's likeness with wiggling fingers.

"No. I mean, yes, but I also helped a student paint his first portrait today and he was delighted. So my degree does a number of things I really enjoy." I should have offered her a glass of wine, but I didn't want to give her any help loosening up to chastise me about dumping Poncy.

"That sounds...charming. I'm sure that trick will be very useful for your student." She wrinkled her nose in a way that said a lot about her actual interpretation of my tidbit.

"It was more than a trick, Mother. It was a breakthrough for him. A connection. A skill addition in his toolbox that he got joy from. It's actually impossible to quantify how important that is." I drained the rest of my wine glass.

She gave me a steely stare like I was talking out of my ass. She was great at that look. Just one sweeping gaze from her and I was reminded how quickly she could deflate me.

Being out on my own had brought out a side of me that she'd been able to bury under her opinions and expectations. I liked doing things that were not weighted down by her outlook on them.

"Who is this man?" Mom pointed at the Bear painting.

"Just another person." I waved my hands around. There was a crowd on my walls.

"Well, Poncy is furious." She tapped the toe of her red-soled heel on my floor. "Do you have your apology ready?"

"No, I don't think I do." I stood from my couch. "Don't you have somewhere else to be?"

The haute seemed to seep out of Mom's nostrils and paint her face. "Of course, I do. But I had to talk some sense into you. I mean, I've already lunched with Poncy's mother, Gretchen. I lunched with Gretchen!" The shrill in her voice alerted me to the fact that I was not going to hear the end of this anytime soon.

"Do you not want to ask what happened? Why I broke up with him?" I walked the wine glass to my sink.

This was the glaring shortcoming. My mother came here worried about Poncy. Man, it was so clear now. Her priorities were wildly obvious.

"I'm sure it wasn't anything huge. I know how you get when it's your time of the month." She perched on the arm of the couch, like sitting on it would ruin her outfit or something. I leaned against the doorframe.

"The Nutwell wedding is not going to happen, Mom. Just let out your disappointment in me. Let's get it over with." I added flourish to my hand and gestured to the spot in front of me.

I watched the seven stages of grief flitter in front of her glare, one after another. And then it looped back down to rage.

"Do you understand how this decision affects me? Not everything is about you, Monday Blue. I have invitations now. The first time I've ever been asked to go to some of the places I've been dying to get into! That's because of the Nutwells. I'm getting to be who I deserve to be." She was spitting mad now.

I had pure joy connecting with Leo today through art. She didn't even care. She'd never understand why that brought me a sense of accomplishment.

My doorbell interrupted us. Mom inserted her wishes into the air like she was hoping to manifest them into truth. "Poncy's come to take you back!"

Infuriating. I was angry with her but also disappointed. Her failings as a mother were so obvious. I walked to the door and opened it wide. Bear was standing there, tool belt cinched low. He was holding a few tools, one that was glowing.

His smile deepened his dimples. It was like whiplash to go from angry with Mom to insanely happy to see this man at my door. His sleeves were rolled up and his tattoos were on full display.

"Is that the man from this tasteless picture?" Mom let herself be known.

Confusion rose on Bear's face. "Everything okay? I just had to check the outlet on your..."

I stepped to him, put my hand around his neck, and pulled him down into a kiss. Then I added my tongue.

CHAPTER 15

BEAR

$\mathcal{M}$y body reacted to Monday immediately. In my brain, I wanted to read the room, make choices. But my arms welcomed her. If Monday wanted a kiss, she'd always get one from me. I put my hands on her hips and slowly stepped her backward so I could close the door behind me.

I had to offer my business brain a small gesture of privacy.

Monday's mouth tasted like wine. A woman that resembled Monday in a more vintage model was tsking in the center of the room.

"You were about to be engaged, Monday! How dare you do this to Poncy. He loves you!" Her mom started hitting me with her huge purse.

Monday pulled away from my lips and held my face in her palms. "That's my mom, Chestnut Level. Ignore her. How was your day, Bear?"

I looked from her mother back to Monday, "Um, pretty standard. Mostly electric. How was your day?"

Monday took her hands from my cheeks and ran them down my arms. "I had the best day. My student was able to communicate his color choices for a portrait of his mom for the first time today. She cried when she picked him up. They are getting the painting framed."

"That's so incredible. I just got chills." And then I really was ignoring the purse wacker, too. "You must feel like a million bucks." I held up a hand when the purse came a little too close to Monday.

"Speaking of a million dollars! That would be about the wedding present total from the Nutwells. And you're throwing that all away for a maintenance man?" The woman was screeching now. "This man has piercings everywhere!"

"Excuse me." Monday turned and caught her mother's flailing purse and yanked it hard. Her mother stumbled and let go.

"What are you doing?" Her mother's face was turning an alarming shade of red.

"The same thing I did last night. Taking out the trash." Monday stomped away from me and threw open the porch door. I heard the distinct plop of a sack hitting the ground.

"Did you just throw my Burberry?" Her mother ran out the front door like she was being chased by someone with a knife.

Monday followed her mother to the door and then swung it closed with a loud slam.

"Is this the way you always say goodbye to guests?" I pointed to her balcony.

She shook her head. "Seems that way. I knew she'd be upset, but I just wanted a few hours to be happy about Leo."

There was more shrieking from outside. I was pretty sure I heard the words *grass stain*. "Well, your mom seems nice."

The brief pause in our conversation was punctuated by her mother's pterodactyl scream.

"She's just so giving and understanding." Monday pressed her hands together as if in prayer.

"How much trouble will you be in?" I dropped the sarcasm. It was hard to see Monday fighting with her mom. It was something I couldn't really understand because my mom and I were so close.

"A lot. But if she wants to be at a Nutwell wedding, she can marry Poncy. I'm not spending another minute thinking about him. We literally dated for two months. I never even slept with him." She went to her porch door and slid some hand painted curtains in front of the glass. "My mom made it out to be way more than it was. She was enamored by the fact that half the buildings in our town have Poncy's last name on them." Her phone was on the table and it started to vibrate. "That'll be my sisters and my father, possibly in that order. Mom will make everyone pay for this decision. Hey, thanks for letting me kiss you. Sorry I had the door open. It just seemed like the perfect way to tell Mom to get lost without saying a word."

"That's cool." I felt the disappointment lick my heart. I didn't want to be a revenge kiss.

"Did you say you need to go on my balcony? I mean, you know the way from the outside, but we can use the door as soon as Cruella de Vil finishes launching her insults at my apartment." We could both still hear her mother's angry voice. I walked over to the painting of me on Monday's wall.

She'd worked on it, she'd told me, since adding the spicy parts to my spicy parts. It was amazing. The color gave texture to the wall that almost made it seem 3D.

My face looked, well, just like my face. I looked a little mad, but my dimples made me seem friendlier.

"Sounds like she finally gave up." Monday opened up the balcony and peeked outside. "Yup. Unless she's hiding, you're all clear out here."

I picked up my tools from off the ground. So that was how it would be. Time to get to work. I walked over to the balcony, and sure enough, Monday's outlet did not have a GFCI button. I tried to refocus on work. Not holding her against my body. Not tasting her wine-flavored tongue. Not feeling her soft breasts pressed against my chest.

This girl was in my head for sure. I focused on her electrical work. I was inspecting her place first because I wanted her to be safe. The safest out of anyone living in the apartments.

It made no sense, mathematically, to start here. I was going to have to turn off this outlet at the fuse box. When I walked back into her place, Monday was sitting on the floor watching a video on her phone.

"Excuse me." I was about to explain that I needed to walk through her place when she held her hand out to me.

"Check this out." She pulled on my hand until I sat next to her. I couldn't see the boy's face because she had blocked it out with a heart emoji.

His movements were abrupt but determined. He picked a button and pressed it.

"Such a huge step for him. I mean, his voice. He's in there, you know? Ready to make choices." She wiped her eyes.

"That's beautiful." And it was. Her care and concern for this student were evident. "Did you show this to your mom?" I'm not sure why it mattered to me, but I wanted to know.

"This? Oh no. I tried to tell her, but she was too busy being disappointed in me." Monday shook her head.

"Well, in my family we'd have a party for you. And we'd invite the kid." That's how Hannings were. We celebrated the stuff that mattered. "That's life-changing for your student. What a great gift to share with that boy's parents."

Monday dropped her hand that was holding her phone. "I wish my mom would see it that way. I swear it's like my soul rings like a bell when we have breakthroughs like this. I live for it. That feeling."

She dragged her index finger down the front of the screen.

She was gorgeous. Monday was traffic-stopping with her looks and style, but this part, crying thinking about this kid? That was so attractive I could barely take it.

"Are you and Poncy for sure over?" I wasn't about to kiss her again.

"It was over before it started, but I didn't have the heart in me to end it. I knew my mother would be disappointed, so I just kept putting the actual conversation off." She leaned over and placed her phone on the coffee table. Then she stood up and I mimicked her movement.

"You're special, Monday." My head was screaming at me, but my body was like a runaway roller coaster. There was chemistry here and I wanted to make it flow.

"I feel like a disappointing dickbag." She turned to face me.

"Anyone disappointed in you isn't paying attention." I stepped closer.

She bit her lip and looked at the floor. "All you've asked is that I cover up that wall and I still have yet to do it." She pointed at the offending mural.

"Listen, we have to discuss the ramifications of that, but I get it. It's a really beautiful painting. I'm flattered, honestly. I mean, this version—the one you took a picture with was a touch..." I trailed off.

She finished for me "...graphic? I get that. I can use these powers for good and evil."

I had to smile. "I did enjoy your outfit, though."

Her cheeks reddened. "That was rage sex clothes."

"Remind me to get you mad again." I crinkled my eyes, hoping to lighten the mood.

"Tell me about the ramifications. I need to know the details." She gestured to the couch.

I wanted to sit with her and tell her everything. But being in her apartment for longer than it'd take to fix the GFCI outlet would be a cause for tongues to start wagging. And in an apartment building filled with windows, I doubt anyone missed a trick around here.

She noted my hesitation. "Maybe some other time?"

"Yeah. Maybe you can come to my place? I don't want to risk being seen out in public and stuff." I shoved one hand into my pocket and pulled out my phone.

"Sure. For sure. Go ahead." She stood and crossed her arms over her chest.

Oh no. I was getting a different read from her. Like she thought she was being rejected for the heart-to-heart. She was staring at the floor near my feet.

I quickly texted her a message. **You can come right now. Follow me in a few minutes?**

Her phone buzzed and she picked it up from the table. "You could've just said this out loud."

She pointed the phone at me.

"I know, but I wanted to make sure I still had the right number. And your walls might have ears." I made a twirling motion with my index finger.

Her eyes narrowed. "You think this place is bugged?"

Now I was making her think I was a conspiracy theory fanatic. "No, it's just that when I'm working in these places, I can hear the neighbors talking as clear as day."

"Okay. I'll follow you out." She shrugged.

So, this was fine. I was going to lead this girl to my place and have it out with her. Right now.

CHAPTER 16

MONDAY

J was sure you were not supposed to go to a second location with a murderer. I'd heard that a number of times at school while growing up. But there was very little information/advice if you insisted on driving yourself to the second location. When I was out on the main road, Bear's work truck pulled in front of me and he flashed his brakes. He was friendly and so sweet about Leo's progress. I got a safe feeling in the pit of my belly when he was around. Maybe I was too focused on the fact that he could control electricity and then made me assign him attributes that didn't actually exist.

He was ridiculously good looking. And he had the perfect amount of tattoos that curved around his arm muscles. Those points shouldn't be a part of my decision-making process, but it was what it was.

While I followed Bear, I thought of Poncy. The feeling of having a weight lifted off of my shoulders was staggering. Whenever I'd forced myself down the wrong path, it felt really great to turn around. Even if it took longer to get where I was originally going.

Bear's blinker signaled and I hissed out loud, "A freaking warehouse? Shit."

That was out of the stalker murder handbook. I still got out of my car when I saw that Bear was smiling at me. And that was setting my body at ease again. He was trustworthy. I knew it. There was a distinct lack of any warning bells in my head.

"Home sweet home." He thumbed over his shoulder.

"Meatpacking sweet meatpacking." I couldn't imagine living in this giant place.

He swung his keys on his finger and then headed to the garage bay. He hit a button on his keys and one of the doors started its slow climb.

He ducked under and slapped on a light, and soon after the garage door was safely tucked away, the light attached to the mechanism went out. "We have to take the elevator."

"Is this where you and your parents live?" It occurred to me that I might be having an unplanned meet and greet.

"No. This used to be my dad's back in the day. Got it real cheap and it was where we kept equipment and some trucks. As I got older, he started selling off the fleet and the extra stock."

Bear put a key into the elevator and then pulled the gate open. I stepped inside with him. The freight elevator was rickety and loud. He mouthed, "Sorry" over the cacophony.

When we were one floor up, I could see the apartment. Well, really a loft. Bear pulled the door open. This was not a normal bachelor pad.

I stepped inside. The art side of my brain hummed happily at all the exquisite furniture in the space. Oak, pine, and cherry-wood were all varnished with a shine. The wood carving tools and cans of stain spoke volumes, but I still asked, "You made these?"

I made my way over to the dining room table with matching log benches.

"Oh yeah. These are my dirty little secrets. My favorite hobby." He hung his keys on a hook on the wall by the elevator.

The table had a channel cut through it. Burned into it. I recognized the jagged legs of electricity even if it was turned off. "You created this part, too?" I ran my fingertip down the elaborate pattern in the center of the table.

"Yeah." He ran his hand through his hair and then shuffled his feet. He was bashful.

"It's incredible." I fell into his art. The wood grain, the way he curved the live edge to respect a particularly unusual knot— it all made sense.

He started telling me stories then, of how he got the wood from different sites over the years. "When I worked with my dad, whenever we went to a house with a lightning strike, which was a lot, he would show me the things the lightning did to objects around the place. And that's where this idea came from."

He grabbed a small piece of sandpaper and absentmindedly ran it over a part of the wood that already looked perfect.

"So you're using wood that's already had this happen to it?" That didn't seem right, because the electric scarring seemed too precise and well placed for that.

"No. I add the electric with a charge. And I aim where it's going to go. I never know for sure how it'll turn out, but I trust the process and it usually picks the best way to go." He knocked lightly on the table.

I went from one piece to another, asking him how he did it.

"I take the table and ready it, then I add an electrical charge and let it burn up the center. I mix together some resin and add it to the top. Then we have a finished table with a Lichtenberg figure pattern." He sat down at the bench that was pulled along-side the table.

"That's terrifying. Have you ever died?" I meant to say *been shocked*. But his uproarious laughter was worth the gaff.

"Not yet. Had a few good shocks that rang my bell, but I'm still here to talk about it." He watched me move about his space. "I'm actually nervous to have a real honest-to-goodness art teacher looking at them."

"It's great, but you know that already. Each piece shows confidence. And I love it. Your medium has me concerned, but the finished products speak for themselves. You're super talented, Bear. Do you sell these?" I sat at the table across from him.

"Nah. I give them to friends and family. My focus is on Hanning Electric, so this is just to blow off a little steam from time to time." I saw a flicker of disappointment in his eyes.

"Speaking of family, do you want to clue me in on what's going on here?" I folded my hands in front of me at the table.

"Okay. Long story short, my father had a heart attack and I'm running his business while he gets back on his feet." He tapped his foot nervously.

"I am so very sorry to hear that. How's he doing?" I felt my eyebrows coming together.

"He's getting better every day. We're grateful to the nurses and doctors at the hospital and now his cardiology team. They were and are amazing." He shook his head, maybe remembering all the moments these medical teams were involved.

"I'm glad. I can't imagine how daunting it must be to recover from an incident like that. So you've taken over his entire business? For how long?" I tilted my head to the side. I could be wrong, but he seemed sad about it.

"As long as it takes. The health bills have really exhausted their savings." He ran a finger down the tree shape on the table.

I covered his hand with mine, stilling the movement. "How's your mom doing?"

Having to worry about the health of a parent hadn't

happened to me, but I imagined it'd be very scary.

"Thanks for asking. Mom's doing a great job being his helper. And he's tough." He looked at our hands.

"So this has to do with me painting your picture how?" I leaned forward, feeling worried that I had really messed this up for his family.

Bear rubbed his temples. "There's a no contact clause in the contract we have with the owner of the apartments concerning the residents. And that painting, well..."

He bit his lip. I finished his sentence for him. "... looks like we contact each other a lot. Naked."

"And it's the naked part that's the real stickler. They want me to have my pants on. Just in general. I'm not sure what the policy is on portraits, but I don't want to ask." He took a deep breath.

"This painting has you worried about your family, your business, and your reputation. Holy crap, I feel like a monster. I'm so sorry." I knew my ears would be red from shame. And now I was getting a kick of heartburn to boot.

"Hey, it's okay. Normally, well, not that this is normal, but I mean, if I didn't find you so attractive I would've just flat out asked for you to paint over it. But you're you..." he smiled, "... and I was flattered, and also the painting is really good. Not the vindictive one with the veins and all, but the one you have right now." He shrugged.

"I'll take a picture of it for you, and then I'll alter the face so it's not recognizable as you. Will that work? Then I won't be wiping it out of existence, just picking a new human to represent." I mentally scrolled through some choices. There had been a guy I saw from the street once that had a super interesting face. I could use my mind's eye picture of him.

"That would solve a lot of issues, for sure. I mean, about the painting. Not about us." He pointed from his chest to me and back again.

"There's an us?" Now it was my turn to point back and forth. Just the thought of it sent a thrill from my toes to my lady parts to the top of my head.

"I'm not willing to give up on kissing you again in the future. That was something I really enjoyed." He touched his bottom lip.

I took a deep breath and the fumes from his workshop tagged themselves to this excitement I felt in my chest.

"I'd like there to be. I mean, if you need time, I'll understand." He moved in his seat, but he was crap at hiding his hopeful face.

I felt a fire inside for Bear, maybe the most intense lust I'd ever encountered. But I did need a bit of time. "I have to process the changes I'm facing. And I get the feeling that you and I would be kind of all-consuming."

There was a part of me—a really big part—that was hoping he might try for a kiss anyway, but he stood immediately. "I understand."

A gentleman. I stood as well. "Let me handle the painting so you don't have to worry about that anymore."

Bear walked me to the elevator as I took a few last lingering looks at his furniture. It was so unique.

"Do you think it'll be okay for you to go back? I mean, is your mom or anyone going to be there?" He pressed the button to get the elevator started. It dropped with a thud that made my knees bend. Bear put out a steadying hand. "Sorry, I should've warned you. This old beast has some quirks."

I pressed his hand against my bicep. "How many more quirks?" I spread my feet a little wider.

"That's it. Just the heart stopping one at the top there. I'm so used to it I don't even notice it anymore."

He patted my arm twice when the elevator had settled on the bottom floor. When he lifted the gate, it made a horrible screeching noise.

Once we were both off the elevator, I answered his question,

"Mom will go back to Dad and complain. He and my sisters might show up, but Mom will stay away until I've apologized."

Bear beat me to the driver's side door and reached for the handle of my car. The key in my pocket had already unlocked the car door. He stepped to the side as he opened my door for me.

"You have to apologize?" His eyebrows met in the middle.

"That's what I'd normally be expected to do, but I swear, moving away from my hometown has really made me question things. Like the Hartford Greens Gala that Mom lives and breathes all year just...doesn't matter here. No one cares." I was stalling and venting at the same time.

"A gala? What for? People really have those?" He stepped closer to me so I had to tilt my head to look up at him.

"It's for fundraising at my parents' country club and being on the chairperson's board is a huge deal for Mom. This year, she promised a ton of things, one of those being a painting from me up for grabs. The winner gets a portrait session with me." I shrugged.

"You've done this before?" His eyes had endless interest in them. He was not only hearing me, he was listening. It felt nice.

"Yeah. Every year since I was fifteen. It's become sort of a status symbol with my mom's friends. They buy some of my time and I paint a portrait of their choosing. Usually they have me do a whole family. But they do give good money to the event cause. And quite a few of those previous bidders helped me get this job with recommendation letters that I added to my portfolio." I leaned into my car and set my phone onto the wireless charger.

"That's awesome of you." He tapped the top of the car door.

"I didn't really have a choice, but now I appreciate that it was a lot to ask a teenager to do. It was always important to my mom." I looked up at the sky briefly. It was crazy how almost every decision I made went through a filter in my brain that could be labeled *family*. I always thought about how what I did would affect my relatives before making a choice.

His phone pinged in his pocket. "Excuse me." He answered it quickly and turned his shoulders away from me. "Everything okay? Yeah, I'm here with Monday--a friend."

I felt like a jerk for whining about my family when his had been through something so incredibly stressful and scary.

"Yeah. No problem. Tell him I'll check while I'm here. Okay. Love you, too, Mom." Bear ended the call and stuffed his phone back into his pocket.

"He's okay?" I was ready to help if Bear needed it.

"Yeah. He has a foldable exercise bike in storage here." He gestured to the warehouse. "And couldn't get the idea of working out at home out of his head until I agreed to bring it to him. I always get nervous when they call me. I mean, I hope that will go away with time, but it really reminds me of that night."

"I think that's totally understandable. And at least, asking for home gym equipment has to be a good milestone to cross." I touched Bear's elbow. "Seriously, I'm sorry that the mural gave you stress. You have enough to worry about."

He looked at my hand for a beat before reaching for it. He ran his thumb over my knuckles. "It's going to be okay, don't worry. We have a great plan."

I shivered thinking of the other places I'd like to have his fingers. He let go and I got into my car quickly before I could turn the simple handholding into something more.

"Can you send me a text when you're home safe?" Bear waited until I was fully seated before closing my door.

After I started the car with the button and rolled down the window, I told him I would.

I hoped I wouldn't regret not pressing for more with Bear. He was silhouetted in my rearview mirror the entire time I drove away and out of sight.

CHAPTER 17

MONDAY

I did text Bear when I got home. It was going to be a long weekend, with much family drama, and I should have been more worried about that. Instead, I went to work on the mural and worked on the face so it was obscured a bit more. You couldn't tell who the man was, just that he was a fit, tattooed man. I snapped a picture and sent it to Bear even though it was an ungodly early hour. I wanted him to rest easy.

I got a thumbs-up emoji in return and then I headed for the shower. I always had a ton of paint to get out from under my fingernails, and by the time I was clean, I was exhausted. I crawled into bed and let thoughts of Bear's tattoos lull me to sleep.

BEAR

By the time I received the updated mural picture from Monday, I had fully researched the Hartford Greens Gala that she spoke of. Each news article gave me a small peek into her past. She was very, very modest about what her paintings brought into the gala fundraising. There was a bidding war each year and the final price tag kept going up and up.

One year, the charity was a local children's hospital. Another, a wildlife preserve. There was yet another news article detailing Monday's mother getting on the board. Then the charities seemed to have a different style of purpose.

Last year, for example, Monday's painting session went to sponsor landscaping at Hartford Greens where the gala was sponsored.

This year, it was to update the golf carts.

Maybe I shouldn't be snooping at all, but with her family name and the word *gala*, I was now wiser to the situation Monday came from. And I had a new appreciation for the yeeting of the purse from the porch. Monday had guts and I liked it.

Hell, I liked everything about her. I was disappointed I didn't get to see her naked, but I got it. She'd had a hell of a night, and I could wait until she was ready. I walked over to one of my oldest pieces of furniture. Dad had actually helped me with this one. I told him about my idea and he'd set aside three whole weekends to help me develop the process safely.

I ran my palms over the resin top. The small bubbles felt like a rustic keyboard. I knew how to make the tops as smooth as hot glass now.

This first table had a ton of memories for me, though, even if it wasn't flawless—it was priceless for me. Dad agreed that just because I had an idea, it was worth putting the time and effort into. A lot of adults would have looked at their kid and told them to take a hike, but not my dad. He always made sure he spent time with me.

After reading about Monday's family and all the things I witnessed with her mom, I knew enough to be grateful for my dad.

I knocked on the table a few times before finally pushing away. Dad had sounded fired up about riding the stationary bike, so I knew I had to get it over to him as soon as possible. The storage garage was packed full to the rafters, so the scavenger hunt was on.

MONDAY

When I woke up, I touched my phone. The motion alerted the device and all of my notifications flooded the screen.

Poncy had sent twenty-three messages. My mother had sent nineteen. My sisters sent ten and nine respectively. And last, but not least, was one message from my father. And that one message was the one I knew meant I was in the most trouble.

I'm headed down for a visit today.

For a Sunday, I knew I was treading on thin ice. Dad usually went golfing with his trio of lifelong friends. They took golf morning very seriously, even, at times, scheduling surgeries and procedures around the tee time.

He'd be calling in sick for his fun time, and that meant his visit would have to be worth it. Mom probably put him up to it. It wasn't long before I heard the doorbell. I stopped dragging my feet and got out of bed. I peeked out the back deck and saw Mr. Nuts dancing there for his breakfast. Thank heavens. It was still very comforting to see Mr. Nuts in the flesh. Well, in the fur. I stared at my front door for a few seconds before my father switched to knocking. He was serious about coming in, whether or not I was ready to face him or not.

I strode to the door, unlocked it, and opened it. Dad was dressed in a pink button-down and white slacks. He had a light-yellow sweater tied around his shoulders.

"Hi, Dad." I held onto the door.

"Princess." He stepped through my apartment door and gave my place a once-over. "Love the murals. These are fantastic." He moved to my side and gave me a hug. I reciprocated it. Here, without Mom, he would be real with me.

He walked closer to the kitchen where I'd recreated an entire family (four generations), working together to keep a restaurant afloat on my wall.

"They are the family that lives in a building two down from this one. They work so hard." I used my knuckle to rub at a small smudge on the wall.

"I can really see their personalities and determination. It's marvelous." Dad tilted his head to the side. "I doubt this was the painting Mom had trouble with."

He walked the length of the place, stopping when he was close to me again to pull me into another hug. When he got to the Bear portrait, he paused. "I bet it's this one." He tapped the bit of white wall next to the now anonymous Bear's elbow.

"She doesn't like anything I've got going on here, so it's a safe bet she hates it all." I sighed, letting my shoulders rise and fall. The same old, same old was destined to happen. I'd get yelled at and I would have to apologize. Then Mom would take her sweet time accepting the apology and I would get stress palpitations.

"She's got a ton of aggravation from planning the gala, you know that. And this was supposed to be the year of the Nutwells." Dad was saying these facts like they were meaningless asides. Like something he'd memorized to say in a poorly funded play.

"Stress she puts on herself. She doesn't have to do it. She doesn't have to do any of this. We could just attend the gala and not be part of any of the hoopla around the event." I kicked the wall, stubbing my toe and scowling.

"We need to figure out the Nutwells' stance on this breakup. I mean, Mom thinks it's quite possible that Poncy won't tell anyone about the split." He folded his arms across his chest.

"You sound just like her. Are you on her side in all of this?" I was incredulous.

"No, of course not, sweetie. It's just the timing is really bad for your mom. So I'm here to plead for you to hear her out. I mean, she's your mother, for God's sake." He held his hands out on either side of his shoulders.

"She wants me to date Poncy still." It all snapped together in my head like a bucket of LEGO bricks. If Poncy didn't tell anyone about the breakup, Mom's society friends would still think Poncy and I were dating. Mom was always playing 4D chess, and half the players didn't even know there was a game going on.

"Not really. I mean, just for the one date—the gala. And the planning weekend, then you can kick Poncy out with the trash for all we care. But Mom really wants this. She's been talking about all the bitches eating crow for months. I don't even know who the bitches are, but I know she wants them to see her daughter become a Nutwell." Dad moved to another mural I had of girls playing jump rope outside my apartment window.

"It's the usual, stuck-up friends she normally tries to impress. I don't even know if those women like each other, or if they just love having someone to worry about being better than."

Dad pushed his mouth to the side. "That may be partly true, but your mom doesn't ask for much. Just a good marriage. She told me to tell you she already has her dress picked out for the wedding, and that it'd be sad if she didn't get to walk down the aisle near you."

"Do you even hear yourself, Dad? This is my life. I'm not just a toy to keep Mom happy. I was dating him for two months. Nine weeks tops. She went into a world of her own." I wanted Dad to leave. Being away from my family and living on my own had opened my eyes to how much the trappings of life that Mom focused on just didn't matter.

I watched as Dad's left eye twitched. I was hitting a mark for him. He was silent for a minute while he chose his internal path. Defend Mom or support me. Dad had to do some elaborate personal comfort gymnastics in his head.

"I'm sorry, Monday. I really am. Things would be easier for all of us if you just did the things you committed to already. I can work on Mom. I see that it's an issue we have to handle. But we have under a month until this event." He took a deep breath that settled his shoulders lower.

I felt my shoulders slump along with his. I had a boundary to set up, but I could compromise. "I'm not going on another date with Poncy. That's a non-starter. But..." Dad's eyebrows lifted like a puppy hearing his favorite word as I continued, "...I'll still do the paint session for the auction."

Dad nodded while tilting his head from one shoulder to another, measuring the outcome. "That'll work. I'll make it work. Can you be discreet about the breakup? Try not to make it obvious if he's not making it obvious?" Dad held out one arm and I walked into him while I answered.

"That shouldn't be too hard. He lives three hours away. I won't change anything on my social media or unfollow him, but I'm not interacting." I gave Dad a squeeze.

"Fair enough. I don't know what half of that means, but I'm thrilled that you're helping me out." He squeezed my shoulders back. "Now, I came all this way, show me around this place, then I'm taking my teacher-daughter out to dinner."

"That'll work." I was happy to show him my small place and he spent a nice long time looking at my paintings. I even convinced him to paint a few things on the spot between the kitchen and the living room. It was hard to say no to Dad, seeing him smile while he painted the start of a tiger on my wall. He really did try to make everyone in our family happy, and I knew for a fact that he denied himself the things that gave him great joy so he could provide for us. I could make his life easier if I could.

And that's why Mom sent him, I realized, as we packed up the paint supplies before dinner. She really was a master at the game. She knew what she wanted, and she knew the moves to pull to get her way.

CHAPTER 18

BEAR

*M*onday morning brought me back to Monday's apartment building. I was there as early as I could be. I worked with Roy to try to get to the apartments as soon as possible. He identified the early risers and people who were out to work already.

Most of the units were okay, save for one or two GFCI plug changes. I happened to see an older man come out of Monday's apartment with her when she was headed for work in the morning. I stayed outside and busied myself at the back of my truck while she hugged the man goodbye and he got into his car.

She was juggling coffee, two bags, and her phone when I eased up next to her, shuffling my feet so she wouldn't be spooked. "Hey."

She still looked surprised to see me. "Hey! You're early!"

"Electricity doesn't sleep." I'd be lying if I said I hadn't hoped I'd get a peek of her this morning.

I offered to hold her cup while she shimmied all her things into her car.

"Thanks," she murmured as she took her cup back. Her fingers touched mine and I was pretty sure my voltage tester picked up the touch as a live wire. Her eyes widened a bit.

"So you had a visitor, huh?" I leaned against her car and took in her appearance. Smooth skin with just a hint of makeup.

"Oh, yeah, that was my dad. Mom sent the big guns to get her way." She wrapped both her hands around the mug of coffee.

"How'd that go?" I was nervous about what that meant for Monday and me. What kind of leverage did her mom have? Certainly, the woman I'd met seemed to have quite a few issues and anger problems.

"It was okay. I mean, having time with Dad is always nice. I'm not sure how much my neck liked sleeping on the couch, and Mom's motives are always suspect." She touched my hand with her warm one. "Did you need coffee? I have some still in the pot. I had to make extra so Dad could have his cup."

I shook my head. "Thanks, I'm good. I have to get back to it. I was just hoping to catch a glimpse of you anyway."

She pulled her phone out of her pocket. "I have to get going, too. I hate to be late to set up for the day."

"Good luck. I hope Leo has more breakthroughs for you." She paused and stared me up and down.

"Thanks. That means a lot. Stay safe today, okay?" Her smile was wide as she got into her car. I waited until she had fully tucked in before shutting her door for her. A hint of her conditioner or whatever special thing she had in her hair hit me. I wanted to bury my nose in that smell until I found her neck to nibble on.

I was down for this girl, hard. I felt like I was supposed to have her. Her kindness and big heart deserved to be in my family. And that was the highest praise I could offer someone.

CHAPTER 19

MONDAY

$\mathcal{I}$ had such a focused day at work and a very long staff meeting at the end of the day that I legitimately forgot about my issues with Mom. I still had the heavy feeling in my chest that told me something was off, but I was just straight-up busy. Leo made huge strides. His mother and father clearly liked working with him at home.

I was sitting in the parking lot of my building while I thought about the connection of color and Leo's new skill set. I really felt that color was a bridge sometimes. Like music was for others, seeing a perfect magenta could be just what was needed to start an imagination and let it run wild.

I picked up all my stuff from the car in a giant scoop. I struggled to see the steps as I managed my way up the stairs. Eventually, I had to plop it down in a pile in front of my door to get it unlocked.

When I was in a nice set of soft sweats with a glass of wine poured, I took a deep breath and powered my phone back on.

The poor thing couldn't stop vibrating for a full two minutes as my notifications pinged in.

All the usual customers made their mark. My sisters, my mother, a sweet note from my dad, and Poncy.

Instead of answering any of them, it was time for girl bonding. I hit the FaceTime button on Radia's contact. Radia had her hair wrapped in a towel and a deep green face mask dried to her skin.

"I'm sorry. I should have texted first. My phone was just blowing the hell up and I didn't want to mess with it." The notification banners were still popping into my field of vision from the top of the screen.

She wrinkled her nose, and it cracked the facemask around her mouth. "Please, we've peed on the same toilet at parties. This is nothing."

I winced, remembering "breaking the seal" with Radia in college. We had drunk-perfected both of us making room for the other so we could pee at the same time. It was a horrible necessity as the lines for the women's bathrooms were always too long.

"That's the truth. The hard peeing truth." I shook my head.

"Those were the days. Man, college makes you do some stuff. What's up, pumpkin pie?" She leaned toward her camera and mushed her lips around to crack the mask even more.

"I have to do the Hartford Greens Gala, right?" She knew. She knew all the drama that went into the gala because her family attended it on occasion. Now granted, her family was on the catering team, but she knew the deal.

"Yeah. That's for sure. They look forward to the session that you offer. It's for charity and all." Radia unwound her towel and I could see a thick paste on her long brown hair.

"Doing a hair salad?" I gently teased her in college when she was doing this treatment. A few times I even got close to her with a fork.

110

"You know me, avocado, mayonnaise, and olive oil keep it silky." She rewrapped her hair.

"I'm going to have to see Poncy." I readjusted my grip so my FaceTime angle was better.

"That's a definite downside of going to the gala. Is there any way you can phone it in?" I watched her answer her own question with a head shake. "Meh. You know they make way more money when you're there."

"Yeah. I haven't really paid attention. I've been so swamped with work." I took a big sip of wine.

"That's a good thing. A real thing. How's the sexy electrician?" She walked me into the bathroom with her and set her phone on the counter.

We'd had many conversations in life with this exact scenario. Radia had always been religious about her skin and hair care. It made sense, though, because her mother looked like her sister with the same routine that had been passed down their generations of ladies.

She started washing the mask off her face, scrubbing hard. I knew it was pointless to talk now. She wouldn't be able to hear me over the water she was sloshing around. I started thinking about our first apartment at college. Like most people, when I told her that electricity had it out for me, she'd laughed. It only took a few months living with me before she swore on everything holy that I was some sort of doomed human.

Wristwatches stopped running on my arm. Cars—perfectly good, new cars—stalled when I was in them, and the computer shut down from my proximity. It'd be a great superpower if it did anything helpful at all. Instead, all it did was make me weird.

When Radia finished drying her face, I answered her question, "Super good. I think. Or I ruined it last night. One or the other."

She was back in her living room now. The hair salad took way longer than the face one.

"What happened?" She was pouring her own glass of wine now.

"Well, he wants to date and I feel like I need to let the corpse of my last relationship get cold before I ride anyone's pointy pony." I swirled the liquid in my glass.

"You owe Poncy not one thing. Seriously. He's such a wanker. I'm thrilled he's gone. And that didn't even last long enough to mourn." Radia was not a big Poncy fan, so I didn't know how biased she was as far as what I owed him.

"Do we know how big the pony is? Like how many hands?" Radia wiggled the fingers on her left hand to illustrate.

"Not yet." I thought about the possibilities for a second.

"That's a dreamy look. I like dreamy." She poked at her hair.

"Tell me about you. This has been the me show." I sat back on the couch.

Radia shook her head slowly. "I've got nothing to be dreamy about. When are you coming home for a visit? Are you not back until the gala? I can't believe I'm still going to that gala. I need to pull a you and get the hell out of here."

"Yeah, I have a long weekend for the gala. Hey, can I stay with you the weekend before? I don't want Chestnut all up in my business. I'm so done with her." That would make her angry. Not being able to pick at me on gala prep weekend while she stressed. Traditionally, anyone involved in the gala had to do basically a rehearsal before to make sure nothing went wrong and everyone knew their place.

"Of course. Your room is always ready. Let's plan on it. You bringing a plus one?" She held her hands out and made her lips into an O shape.

"Just you." I tipped my glass at her. "If you'll have me."

"Oh my gosh, we're going to dress so hot. So hot. We're going to melt their faces off. Revenge dressed. I love it. Come early. We can shop." She rubbed her palms together.

"It's on."

Radia and I finished our wine and then said goodbye. She was a perfect stress reliever. I felt like pre-planning my stay at her house would for sure make my next few weeks more tolerable.

My phone pinged with another text. Bear.

How'd it go today with your student?

So great. His parents worked with him over the weekend. I think his favorite color is green.

Imagine that! You got to know his favorite color. That's amazing. Who knows what else he'll share now that he has that outlet.

I let the warmth of Bear's attention seep up from my toes to my heart. He realized that this was important to me.

How was the rest of the apartment complex? Are we less likely to burn down now?

Far less likely. I'll be back tomorrow, too. See you at your car.

I sent him a smiling emoji and headed to the kitchen to tackle dinner. I knew I had the makings of a salad and a can of biscuits, so that seemed like a low fuss meal. Thinking about seeing Bear in the morning definitely changed my mood. Eventually, I would have to deal with the family upheaval, but I made sure to respond to my father, so everyone knew I was fine, just quiet.

My salad and a reality show were all I worried about for the rest of the night.

THE WEEKS LEADING up to the gala were chock-full of Bear in the mornings. He met me at my car, or sometimes on the stairs to help with my bags. I brought him coffee out as well. We kept it light and respectful.

At night, I could reliably get a text in the evening.

Check out how the ink flowed in the resin!

I hit the play button on the video. The table Bear was working on resembled the edge of a beach. He added a touch of blue that gave a real motion to the liquid, even when it was dry.

That's incredible! How are your parents doing?

I kicked my feet up on the ottoman by my couch.

So good. Dad went to the grocery store with Mom today. Super great to see him out and about.

He's a fighter. Just like his son. I sent a winky face, thinking of his Poncy punch.

How were your kids today?

I took the opportunity to share a few pictures of the kids' work.

Bear reacted to each image with different, excited emojis. Followed with a text: **You're going to have to set up a gallery for them.**

I smiled at how much he got it. He knew that this made me happy. I filed through some extra pictures and found the album I had hidden behind a calculator app. I had a few steamy snaps from my last bath. I sent him a vanishing text of one of my favorites.

Thank you for being amazing.

Noooo. It disappeared. How could you do that to a man?

He sent me a picture of his face looking forlorn.

I resent the picture without the special feature this time so he could keep the image.

Now that makes my night.

I bit my bottom lip and then tapped out another message. **I think we should have a trade here.**

I like things to be fair, so...

There were a few seconds and then I had my very own

special vid. Bear had a short video clip of his face, then a quick drop down on his bare chest and abs.

I sent back: **Lucky me. I know I'll have sweet dreams tonight.**

Same here, beautiful. Sweet dreams.

The texts from Bear were a great distraction from the fact that I was exclusively responding to my father's text messages. I managed to not open anything from my mother or sisters in weeks. I only saw the first little preview of their text messages.

It felt freeing to force the space I needed.

I recognized that being three hours away was a huge help in this regard. The snowy weather was also a bonus. No one wanted to travel when there was a pretty good risk of snow or ice. There hadn't been any need for school closures yet, just enough to cause a pause in a road trip.

I was mum on Poncy. I didn't change anything on my social media, but during the doldrums of winter, I had to really kick it up a notch at school. The kids loved adding color to their days when the landscape was white and gray.

I even did a whole week themed in the tropics.

Leo had a few setbacks, and then he had a week home with a cold. But the tropics week really got him excited again. He did a picture of a parrot and really went all out changing the colors of the feathers with his button.

Time moved on, though, and the night of the gala was fast approaching. I had responded to the official invite from the board, saying that I was donating my services to the auction. I also decided this would be my last year. I let them know that as well so they had ample time to find another artist to do the session before next year.

I was making strides on my own. I just hoped a trip back to my old stomping grounds wouldn't mess with my new confidence.

CHAPTER 20

BEAR

 he slow build with Monday was my speed. I mean,
don't get me wrong, I wanted things to advance
with her, but my heart was a slowpoke. It liked easing into
things. As long as she was still interested, and I guessed that
she was judging from our fairly deep text conversations and
the megawatt smile she gave me when she saw me in the
mornings.

I was almost done with her building, though, and I had really
come to depend on the rush of seeing her every day. I was at
Mom and Dad's for dinner when he mentioned the gala that
Monday was donating her services to.

"I hear they want a really complicated setup and Burnie
reached out to me to see if you were interested in helping out."
Dad ran his thick forefingers in circles on the table. "I know the
apartment buildings are almost all up to code, so a new job
might be welcome. It's a bit of a ride, though."

"What are they looking at?" I was reluctant to commit to

something so far away from Monday even if it was her hometown.

"He was mentioning synching some LEDs with music. Remember when you did that last Halloween for the grocer downtown?" Dad stabbed a green bean with his fork.

"I can manage that. How many days will he need me?" I cut a small piece of turkey.

Mom piped in, and I was grateful because I didn't want Dad jumping into work too soon, "When I took the call, Burnie mentioned a consulting trip this weekend and then again the weekend of the event."

"That's good. I should be done with the apartments by Thursday evening barring any unforeseen problems." There was a weird undercurrent to our dinner. Like really odd. I decided to stay quiet and see if my silence shook anything loose from my parents.

It only took about five minutes before my father was clearing his throat. "Son, I wanted to talk to you about something." He put down his fork with a clang.

I set mine down, too. Fear came over me. I immediately thought of his heart and his health.

Mom, being the intuitive person she was, put me out of my misery. "It's about business."

"Oh. Good." I took a deep breath, feeling my shoulders loosen.

"It might be time for me to retire." Dad folded his fingers together and peered at me.

I nodded. "I think that's a smart decision. It's totally time for you and Mom to live it up."

"Hanning Electric has been in the family a long time. And I wanted to offer the business to you."

This was a big moment. Possibly coming a good three to four years sooner than Dad had planned before the heart attack. And it was a lovely gesture. I knew I should be grateful. Very few people had an established business handed to them. The thought of taking on the whole show for good felt like someone had a vise grip on my windpipe. Claustrophobia and impending doom served themselves up on my dinner plate next to my food.

"Thank you." I nodded.

"We've got time, obviously. And I know you have your hands full at the moment, but I'd love for us to make a plan for the transition when your load lightens a little." Dad gave me a big smile before picking up his fork.

He hadn't heard whether or not I was going to accept or not. Only an idiot would turn this down. Running electricity through furniture as a design was not a career path.

The universe had set me up to help at Monday's gala the same night Dad had moved a few steps closer to retirement. I should take it as a sign. I tried to match Dad's jovial mood, but I caught a few side-eyes from Mom. She knew what was up. Maybe even better than I did.

AFTER DAD WAS TUCKED into bed, Mom came down to the living room to chat. She tucked her feet under her before sitting next to me on the couch. She didn't say anything. All she did was rub my back. We stayed like that for a little while before I spoke up, "He was so happy about the retirement option."

"He's happy about it. Hanning Electric feels like a gift to give you for him. It solved a lot of issues for your father and me when we were first married. It has a legacy attached to it, but…"

She changed from rubbing my back to patting it. "You may have a different dream, and that's okay. Since your father's incident, I've been making sure to keep things low stress for him.

When he came up with this idea, his blood pressure went down. Literally, I watched it drop when I took his vitals earlier."

"Then I've got to do it. If it helps Dad, you know I'll do anything." I sighed.

"The last thing your father or I want is you saddled with a responsibility that hinders you from living the life you picture for yourself." She put both her hands in her lap.

It was comforting being with her. Mom always made me feel safe. Even when navigating the harsh realities of everyday life, with her I knew I'd figure out the answer to whatever was bothering me.

"So what do you want to do?" She leaned forward so she could see my face.

"I don't know honestly. Which makes me feel like the decision should be an easy one. Steady money, a business to call my own. I can be here near Monday, and I really like where that's headed, I think." I rubbed my knees.

"But you want something else. Something riskier." She summed up in seven words exactly the feeling I was having trouble pinning down.

"Yeah. Maybe."

Mom traced a tattoo on my wrist. "You know when you started doing these, I knew you wouldn't be taking on the business."

"I got my first at eighteen. How is that possible?" Now it was my turn to peer at her face.

"I don't know. It was just something so very...you. And then you kept adding to them, and getting things pierced. Making yourself into art. I just think what makes you happy will be off the beaten path." She patted my hand and stood. "I have to get to bed. Are you staying with us tonight?"

I had my old bedroom set up as a place to crash. It had just made sense as I slipped into Dad's role at Hanning to be right here in the heart of it all.

"Yeah. I'm beat as well, and I have some thinking to do." I stood next to Mom and held out my arms for a hug.

She gave me a warm one. "Just know Dad and I are so proud of you. No decision will be the wrong one if you do what you need to do for yourself. And I'm glad to hear about Monday."

I watched as she walked upstairs. I appreciated what she had said, but the part of me that was always going to be concerned for my parents was really loud in my head. I needed to protect Dad. A constant stream of revenue would guarantee that we'd all have a fighting chance with the bills if he had any complications.

I wasn't about to abandon Dad and Mom.

MONDAY

Texting with Bear was a highlight of my day but mentioning that I had to drive home for a gala meeting got me an unexpected bonus: a traveling companion.

It turned out that Bear was working with the company that was managing the tech for the show as a contractor. Something about LED lights. He had a hotel room, but it seemed to make sense for us to take the ride up together. Radia made very elaborate faces when I told her about it.

"Are you going to make your move?"

"Maybe." And the truth was, I couldn't stop thinking about making my move. Bear's official work for the apartment was coming to a close. He'd still be on hand for emergencies, but he wouldn't be walking me to my car in the morning.

I knew he would keep pumping the brakes until I told him

exactly how I felt. He was a good one. A gentleman. And seemingly interested in me as a person. It was refreshing.

Mom had stopped texting and trying to call. It was both a relief and terrifying in equal measures. I was in new territory. Not listening to Mom, not trying to make her happy was foreign. I'd see her this weekend for the dress rehearsal/meeting. It'd be in a public setting, so she would be on her best behavior. With my plans to travel with Bear and stay at Radia's, there was a possibility that I could miss out on the big battle I knew was brewing right under the surface.

Friday morning, after setting out extra food for Mr. Nuts, I met Bear at my door with my suitcase.

We were both grinning when we locked eyes. He was so dreamy. When he flirted, his dimples popped up when his smile was particularly wide. It was everything I was looking forward to.

He asked for my suitcase, and I locked my apartment door. The paint was still wet. I had redone it—yet again—with a broken glass motif.

"Love it." Bear stopped to take a picture.

"Thank you." I'd experimented with holographic paint and a bit of glitter. It was effective as the morning sun hit the door.

"Can I get a picture with you next to it?" He lifted a hopeful eyebrow.

My blush was going to be slightly darker than I intended with my makeup. I pointed to the door and stuck out my tongue.

"Perfect."

I was delighted to see him set it as his wallpaper.

I had a really, really good feeling about this weekend with Bear. It was such a clash with my family situation. It was like finding a treasure chest in a monsoon.

We walked down to his truck, which made sense to drive because he probably had to take his tools and stuff. My mother's voice was in the back of my head, that I would be essentially traveling around in a work truck. I refused to let her judgmental voice ruin my happy.

Bear opened the passenger door for me and held out his hand so I could climb in. Afterwards, he put my suitcase in the back. As he backed the truck up, he put his arm around my seat, and I turned to look at him.

"Hey, pretty." He smiled again. My heart did a fluttering thing, like it had been sleeping and was finally awake.

"Hey." His smile matched mine.

When he put the truck in gear, he paused and took my hand. He slowly lifted it to his lips and gave my knuckles a quick kiss.

This weekend was going to be both amazing and horrible. I was really looking forward to the amazing part.

CHAPTER 21

MONDAY

*W*e stopped for brunch once we were in my town. I directed Bear to a diner and he had to back his truck into a spot.

He held out an arm and I took it as we headed inside.

"This was the place to be in high school." I unwrapped my scarf and Bear took it and my jacket from me to hang it with his on the hook by the booth.

As if to illustrate my point, a loud group of teens clamored in and took up a huge round table in the back.

After we were seated, I directed Bear to the table where the menu was embedded in thick varnish.

"I highly recommend their hamburgers and shakes. They even have a burger with a scrambled egg on it." I pointed the items out with my index finger. He lifted my hand to his lips again.

The server came by and added her opinion, "The cutest. Please tell me this is the first date?"

She had a high, bouncy blonde ponytail and dark red lips.

"Sort of." Bear shrugged his shoulders and his eyes twinkled.

Oh, it was on like Donkey Kong. The ending of the apartment work had freed up some reservations he had, I was guessing.

Bear ordered what I suggested and I got a matching meal. After the server had placed our water glasses, we knew we had a few minutes to ourselves.

"Sort of a date, huh?" I sipped my water and the ice clinked on the side of the glass.

"If that's okay with you? I've had the best time with you in the mornings and I really found myself worrying that we won't spend time together anymore." He shot a look over his shoulder and then rested his hopeful gaze on me.

"It sounds super okay to me." We soaked up the surroundings as we waited for our food. The high schoolers were loud and flirty.

"What were you like in high school?" I ran a finger down the side of my glass, making space in the condensation.

"Quiet. I liked to not make a fuss. I did my homework and then got home to do real work with my dad and grandpa." He mimicked me, drawing on his glass. "I bet your experience was very different."

"It was and it wasn't. What Mom made us do wasn't considered work, but it was required. We'd fight with her. She'd fight with us. There were expectations we had to meet. And we always fell short. I loved art. She loved the idea of being in high society." I quieted down because the server brought us our food.

I heard Bear moan at the sight of the burger. The smell of the food hit me next and reminded me I was hungry as well.

We literally spoke in grunts and moans while we ate for the first few minutes.

Bear circled back to the high school conversation as soon as we were both slowing down. "Hey, I feel like my question came off wrong. I guess I figured with your fancy upbringing it would be all about parties and great gifts. I'm sorry it was hard for you."

He reached out his hand and touched my wrist.

"Thanks. For years I would've laughed it off, the thought that my upbringing was hard. But now that I'm farther away from all of it, I think there was some damage there." I covered his hand with mine. "So, tell me what you're thinking about for your job here? Are the LEDs a problem to work with?"

I was treated to the inner workings of programming the lights. Bear explained his ideas for adding some magic to the winter wonderland theme. He'd researched some ideas and would be taking notes during the meeting today.

Bear paid our bill, though I offered to split it.

"You can get next." He held out his hand to me as we walked out.

My hand fit in his so well. Something so simple made me just a puddle.

He helped me into the truck, and we headed to the hotel first for Bear to check in before he drove me over to Radia's place. I didn't want this pretty delicate bud of a relationship to have to face the firehose of my mother's ire. I was really regretting agreeing to any part of the gala at all.

CHAPTER 22

BEAR

*A*fter Monday and I arrived, we had to separate. The auction participants had a breakout group on the top floor of the Nutwell Blissful Convention Center, also known as the NBCC. I was meeting Burnie and his crew in the back near the electric panel.

I shook hands with all the guys there and told Burnie I'd give my father his best. There were challenges with the building. Some of the wiring was suspect and we'd have to check it before the meeting. We didn't want to agree or plan for anything that the electrical grid on its own couldn't support safely.

After I slipped into the banquet hall with my voltage tester, I made a point to sidle along the wall and make notes of what I found. I saw Monday's mother from a distance. She was far too involved to notice me. Gone was the angry face and the harsh lines from our last meeting. Now she was grand and laughing with her head tipped back. It was like a ballet of bullshit, I was betting. These women spent half their conversations leaning close to another and whispering about each other.

"Chestnut, I saw Monday upstairs. It's lovely to see her in the flesh. Such a shame she's already bowed out for next year." The woman speaking had her hand splayed on her chest with her thumb and index finger framing a large gem on her necklace.

Chestnut's mouth looked like a split slug and her eyes went cold. "Ferra, so wonderful of you to notice her. If you've taken such an interest, I expect you'll be the high bidder on her portrait session."

Ferra laughed too loud while looking around. "I'd hate to take the experience from someone else that actually has room for her pictures. My art is already mounted." Ferra's shoulders moved up and down as if they were on mini carousel horses.

"Of course. How thoughtful of you." Chestnut pulled her chin up and used her nose like a sharpshooter taking aim.

I moved to the next outlet.

"Is Poncy going to propose at the event? It'd be so lovely." Ferra let her hand fly about like she was having trouble controlling it.

Chestnut's demeanor got even colder. How that was possible, I wasn't sure.

"Oh, Ferra. Let's not get into the affairs of the young. We have a big enough job here." The tall woman behind Chestnut glided forward. I hadn't noticed her before and had a hunch she'd been hanging back.

"I just want to make it to another Nutwell wedding. Anthony's was such an event." Ferra let her voice go deep as if she was still impressed.

From the context clues, I was guessing the tall woman was related to Douchebag Poncy. When I squinted, I took an educated guess that the tall woman was his mother because she looked like him in a wig.

His face looked way better on a lady. I slipped over to the next outlet, getting even closer to the group of women.

"I bet that's true, darling. You made off with three centerpieces. You love adding to that collection." The tall woman put her hand on Ferra's shoulder and encouraged her to laugh.

Oh, I was betting Nutwell had the most money in the room. The women seemed to defer to her.

This weekend was going to be tough on Monday. The truth had yet to be revealed about the Poncy breakup. Monday's mom was still riding the fake engagement rumor train.

I had one last outlet to inspect before I was met in the middle by another guy on the crew. We compared notes and then headed out.

The group of women reminded me of when I fed seagulls French fries in the Walmart parking lot. They all hung out together but didn't seem like friends.

I pulled out my phone and sent a text to Monday. **Overheard some stuff about Poncy. Watch out, they are talking like you guys are still together.**

I got a message back right away. **Oh, thanks. Glad to see everyone is all screwed up about it. I've been asked three times why I wasn't wearing my ring. Mom and I are going to have a conversation tonight and I'm not looking forward to it.**

I'm here for you.

I was not used to these kinds of dynamics, with hostility. But as I pondered Dad's business, I knew everyone had hurdles to manage with family.

We had to sit in on the meeting, and that was the first place I saw Monday. There was a lunch snack buffet. When some of the workers started grumbling about wanting to get some food, Burnie held up a hand. "As soon as the meeting's over, I have pizza being delivered downstairs. So sorry about the timing."

Monday waved at me while putting together a salad and a biscuit. She sat at a table with a varied group of people—some who looked slightly out of place. A text message pinged through.

This is the artist's table. They like to keep us together and far away from the fancy ladies.

As everyone filtered through, all the guys at my table, which was on the left toward the back, stayed put.

The committee of ladies that had been bickering before were seated at a table on a dais with microphones.

Poncy in a wig tapped her mic before addressing the crowd. "Now that we are all prepared, I'd like to thank you for coming today, and for all you do to help the country club. This year, we are upgrading the golf carts and adding bidets to all the toilets. It'll be a wonderful event." The placard in front of her proclaimed that she was Mrs. Nancy Nutwell, president.

I felt my phone ping again. I pulled it out discreetly and checked the screen. **Why are you not getting lunch?**

Bossman said no can do. We're not allowed.

I slid my phone back into my pocket as Monday read her screen. I watched as the frustration and anger flitted over her pretty face. She was getting riled up. Then she started whispering to the lady next to her. About half of the artists stood in tandem from their table. They started plucking whole food trays and bowls from the buffet.

The older artist women in flowing skirts started wordlessly directing the servers positioned around the room.

Soon, my table of electricians and techs, the maintenance workers' table, and the staff of the country club had food, plates, and glasses. Monday placed my plate, which came pre-served with a thick slice of cherry pie.

Through her smile, she whispered, "They're jerks."

Eventually, even the composed Nancy Nutwell had to stop

and take note of all the movement. "Mindy and Monday? Is everything okay?"

She had verbally picked those two out of all the shuffling crowd.

Monday lifted her hand and spoke in a haughty voice I'd never heard her use before. "So sorry. I just have trouble eating my lunch in front of people not eating lunch. Surely leaving everyone out was an oversight."

I watched Chestnut instead of Nancy. Her eyes grew wide and I wasn't entirely sure she was breathing. Then I watched Nancy grace Chestnut with a withering glare. "Of course, dear. I'm sure your parents will be glad to cover the cost."

I stood up. "I'll cover the cost. Send me the bill."

I forced myself to maintain eye contact with Mrs. Nutwell instead of trying to tally up the amount of food that was now spread out over six giant tables.

"And you are?" She slid her reading glasses down to the tip of her nose.

"Bear Hanning, ma'am." I nodded at her. I had no place offering this up. And it was stupid. But I wanted to defend Monday if I could. Even if it was a roundabout way.

"Very well. That's terribly kind of you, Mr. Hanning. I'll get your information after lunch. I hope everyone enjoys the meal." She gave a sweeping gesture to the room. I felt Monday put her hand on my shoulder as I sat. She leaned down to my ear and whispered, "We're having wild sex after this."

My concerns about the bill melted in my head and my man brain was instantly wondering how all of her clothes were fastened. I wanted to have a plan. I needed a plan.

Damn, screw the plan. She was biting a smile as she sat back down. I wondered if I had imagined what she had said, but she fluttered her eyelashes and then licked her lips.

Oh, it was happening.

The event information was long and drawn-out. Clearly,

these women spent a lifetime on the minutiae of the event. Who spoke, where they walked, the dance floor situation. I took notes as I ate. I got a few back slaps from other lunch receivers as they passed by, which was fine. I'd figure out the cost later. After sex with Monday.

MONDAY

After lunch was over, I had a few words that needed to be shared with Mrs. Nutwell. She was in a huddle with her committee members. When she saw me approach, her eyes held a numerous amount of feelings that were easily read. Contempt, disapproval, and I thought I saw a bit of fear.

And that was fair. I knew my painting session was the biggest moneymaker for this event, and the fact that it'd be the last one had started up a lot of pre-gala buzz. Radia had told me there had been a few arguments among the influential families about who was entitled to buy my last session.

I had some leverage, and I was about to use it all. "Mrs. Nutwell, can I trouble you to talk briefly?" I gave a long, deliberate look up and down the table, passing my mother as well. "Alone?"

Nancy Nutwell's mouth formed the letter O. Actually, it was somehow a capital letter.

"Well, this is unusual. Whatever you want to say to me you may say in front of the committee. We all work together on this gala."

I wanted to point out that actually she wasn't working with the technicians and the country club employees when she was forcing them to watch her eat lunch, but I had a different goal and decided not to bring it up.

"For sure, this is the perfect place to discuss what I'm going to bring up right now." I folded my hands and gave her a judgmental smile. I tapped my bare left hand on my elbow. The rumor about Poncy and I getting engaged was like a ghost haunting the movement.

Maybe it was my wording or remembering that her son and I were not actually involved anymore, but she stood and came around the table. "No need to be vulgar, girl."

"Not one thing I've said to you has been vulgar." I was starting to draft some spicier replies in my head.

Mrs. Nutwell motioned for me to follow her to an empty corner of the event space. When we were finally settled in our face-off positions, she tried to set the tone. "I'm a very busy woman, and this is a huge event. I really don't have any time to waste." She tapped her expensive watch to emphasize her displeasure.

"That's great. I'm really happy for you. As you well know, or as you *should* well know, Poncy and I aren't dating anymore. I'm happily keeping my mouth quiet about that because somehow it matters to my mother. But I want you to understand I am one hundred percent ready to throw this whole gala under the bus if you force that electrician to pay for the buffet. The fact that you assumed that the people who work their tails off to help us with events like this don't deserve the same treatment as the debutantes that plan parties really irritates and offends me." I switched my weight from one foot to another and rubbed my palms together.

Mrs. Nutwell's gaze lifted. My mother stepped next to me.

"I'm so very sorry, Nancy. We'll take care of that bill. This is truly an oversight on my part."

"Did you know about Poncy and Monday?"

My mother nodded. "Of course, I knew. Poncy and I stay in

contact. Every couple has their ups and downs. If you'll excuse me, Nancy, I have to talk to my daughter."

Oh, my mother was playing the long game, for sure. I felt my teeth clap together hearing that she had been in contact with Poncy. She should've been on my side. She should've been loyal to me.

My mom grabbed the top of my arm and squeezed, and it froze my tongue as if it had happened when I was younger. When Nancy slipped back to the committee table, I turned to my mother and made eye contact with her for the first time since coming back to town.

"You're talking to Poncy? How is that even possible? You never fail to disappoint me, Mom." Even I was a little surprised at my tone. But living away from her had really given me a nice strong backbone, it appeared.

"You listen here. I have a lot on the line. I've been working this event for decades. And for the last ten years having my daughter have an item that was the top seller was a point of pride. It actually helped me get on the committee. And now you're here ready to blow it all up. Never mind that you told everybody that you weren't going to paint next year without consulting me. Now you're here blackmailing Nancy? Let me tell you this when you're away at your teaching job playing house with your electrician. My life here will still be important to me, and I won't have you sabotaging me. I'm your mother."

I knew I shouldn't be focusing on the ropes of tendons in her neck, but I was really thinking about putting my hands around them and squeezing.

"You literally see this whole world as your stage and you're the main character in it. I'm just a side character for you to get the things you want. I'm so glad you have my sisters, and I'm this close to telling you to take a paintbrush and stuff it in your piehole. I keep my commitments and I did commit to do this so I will do it, but so help me, I want you to stay far away from me."

133

I actually saw a tinge of remorse when I told Mom to stay away. And the little girl in me tripped in my confident delivery. I spun on my heel and headed back to Bear's truck. Participating in this was probably not the best idea. At least I had the sex I threatened Bear with to look forward to.

CHAPTER 23

BEAR

onday looked both beautiful and depressed at the same time. I walked closer to the truck, carrying my toolbox. She had her back against the door with her arms folded. When she saw me, her lips picked up in the corner, making a tiny smile.

"What happened in there?" I hefted the box into the back after swinging open the door.

She stepped toward me as I closed it up. "I think I told my mom off."

I held open my arms to her. No matter how angry Monday felt at her mom, it couldn't be easy to yell at her.

"You wanna head over to my hotel and talk about it?" I rubbed her back.

"That'd be great. Yes, please. I would very much like to get out of here." Monday twirled in my arms and I walked behind her to hold open her door. After she was secure, I shut it.

I'd waited for the bill to arrive from Mrs. Nutwell, but the rest of my day didn't hold her in it at all. I glanced at Monday and she looked forlorn. When we got to the hotel, I saw a few other guys from the crew. We were going to have a big day tomorrow planning the faux snow and huge lit up trees that would decorate the hall. I needed to meet with the sound coordinator tomorrow as well. I excused myself to firm up a few details. When I returned to the truck, Monday was holding her phone.

"Everything okay?" I motioned to her screen.

"Yes, just telling Radia where I am. I have plans for us to join her for dinner. But I wasn't sure if you wanted to go upstairs and let me fulfill the promise I made." She tilted her head.

And man, did I. My pants were immediately interested in hitting the floor and finding out everything Monday had to offer, but the sadness in her face dialed me down a few notches.

It didn't make sense to take this big of a step in our relationship squeezed in between a fight with her mom and dinner with her friend. I was sure the release would be amazing, but I wanted a chance to savor her. I also didn't want to let her to think I was rejecting her either. I appreciated what she was offering, and I liked where her head was going, too.

I opened her door and she slid out. "I'm getting used to all this door stuff." She was trying to lighten the mood.

"Can I grab my suitcase? I'll need a few things there." She walked to the back of the truck.

I opened it and unfurled the handle so the suitcase would roll for her. We walked together to the elevator and I hit the button for level three and we were quiet until the door revealed the floor. Room 343 was a bit of a walk, but the room was clean and inviting once I had the door closed.

Before we had the door open, her mouth was on mine. All my gentleman's plans went up in smoke. She dropped her bag and hopped into my arms, straddling my waist as I stood in the wreckage. Kissing Monday was blowing my mind. I kicked her bag so it would roll into the room and let the door swing shut.

MONDAY

I was betting he could hold me all day long. His arm and back muscles were defined and hard. Holding up a woman didn't even make him groan. His lips were so plump and knowledge-able. He added the tip of his tongue before I could think of it. Oh, he knew how to kiss, like really kiss. We moved toward the bed, and he swung me around so I was on his lap when he sat down.

I wanted to be on his lap. I started on his shirt buttons while he kissed from my jaw to my neck. The tattoos. They were so much better than I imagined. After sex, I'd take a big gluttonous gander at his skin under a strong light. Someone who really understood tattoos had done him.

"Your art—I get to kiss it. I love it." I ran my hands down his chest, learning the ridges of his muscles.

The sexy, heady look on his face made me smile. I was so, so excited to see the rest of his body, and I was particularly inter-ested in the part I was straddling. Nothing about this man was going to be disappointing.

He held me by my hips.

The very loud sound of a FaceTime call ringing from my purse stopped us cold. We looked at each other while we waited for it to taper off.

Eventually, it ended. And then just as we started began kissing again, it started back up.

He squinted his eyes at me. "Any hunch who that is?"

We returned to our make-out session, but the FaceTime didn't stop. Over and over until I sighed.

"How much battery does your phone have left? Maybe it'll die." He let go of my hips and kissed the end of my nose.

I reluctantly went to my purse and dug for the glowing screen. It was my mother. Over and over and over.

"It's Mom." I declined the call.

"Everything okay? I mean, like there's no medical issue, right?" And then I knew he was thinking about his father's heart attack. I thought about how upsetting it must have been. It would seem a bit callous for me to at least not check.

The next time it rang through, I answered it.

"Monday! Where are you? I've been looking for you every-where. Did you leave? Are you not planning on staying here with us? Is that a hotel?" Mom tried to look around my head.

"Everyone okay? Like health wise?" I bit my top lip, already annoyed that I had to explain every damn thing to her.

Just behind my mother, Poncy appeared. He was with her at their house. Mom turned to show Poncy that I had answered my FaceTime. I happened to see my father, my sisters, and their husbands all sitting at the dinner table.

"Are you kidding me? Are you having a family dinner with Poncy? Holy crap. I can't deal with this." I ended the FaceTime call and then powered down my phone completely.

I put the phone against my forehead.

"Hey." Bear took the phone gently from my hands and set it on the end table.

I shook my head slowly as he wrapped me in his arms.

"I shouldn't have pressed you to answer. That's me putting my stuff on you. I'm sorry." He gently stroked my hair.

"You have a good soul and are a great son. That was common sense advice. My mother is...something else. I'm so angry." I made my hands into fists and rested them on his shoulders.

"You want me to go kick Poncy's ass again?" He ran his knuckle down my jaw.

"Yes. And I want to video it and watch it on repeat." I laughed a little at the thought.

He hugged me closer.

"Well, that was a mood ruiner." I glanced at the clock. "We have to leave in a half hour. I can probably buy us some time if I text Radia."

Bear wrapped his hands around my wrists and slowly removed them from his shoulders. "Sit down for me. We need to have an important discussion."

I felt my stomach drop. This was it. He'd seen too much craziness up close. I'd scared him away.

He knelt in front of me as I perched on the edge of the mattress. "We can have sex. Amazing, hard sex. My man business is always going to be involved in his head with you." He gestured to his crotch with one hand and grabbed my other hand.

"But something about this seems super special. Like I want you to have me on my A game and vice versa. I want to be special. I want to be impossible to ignore or make an excuse for. I want you to feel like the world is ending and beginning right here between us. When it feels like that for you, you tell me and I'll come to you wherever you are." Bear kissed my knuckles.

I felt tears in my eyes. It was like he was proposing to me with his dick. I loved it.

"I feel that way, too. I mean, I really, really want you, but it does feel special. You feel special." I reached out with my other hand and put it against his cheek. He turned his head and placed a kiss in the center of my palm. "Okay. Let's save my promise for a different time in the future. Possibly the very, very near future."

He gave me a huge smile. "Yes. Let's make sure our first time is all about our first time."

I hugged his head to my chest and that position led to even more making out. As we got ourselves hot and bothered, Bear stood and stepped backward.

"Okay, any more of that and I won't be able to think straight."

"Same here." Actually, I was already thinking crooked. "Let me freshen up for dinner."

I righted my suitcase, unzipped it, and slipped out my toiletries bag. I kissed him twice more but made sure to keep my hands to myself.

When I closed the bathroom door, I could feel my heart beating hard in my chest.

Bear was right. This was different. So different it seemed like the start of forever. Just maybe.

CHAPTER 24

BEAR

*R*adia was charming and hilarious. I did my best to take my eyes off Monday. She got prettier by the second, I swear.

We were all sharing a family style offering of chicken parm in an Italian restaurant that Monday and Radia proclaimed the best in the world. Red wine was flowing and the dull roar of conversation kept up the buzz.

"So remember that time we were both locked out of the dorm in our pajamas?" Radia was scrolling through her phone.

"Yes. That's random and a million years ago." Monday leaned forward to see the screen Radia was sharing.

"Well, Rich sent me a picture today. Remember when they were torturing us because they were the only ones that we could get to come to the window?"

"They took pictures? Those assholes." Monday took the phone and scrolled through some pictures.

I leaned over to take a peek. Monday's hair was shorter and

standing pretty much straight up. Both she and Radia had on short shorts and tank tops. I was guessing from the snowy environment that they were super cold.

"Wow. I hope they let you in. That looks uncomfortable." I took a sip of wine. Obviously, they'd survived.

"They did. We had to agree to date them, which we never did, to get them to open the door." Radia took her phone back and laid it screen side down next to her.

"So why were you out there in the first place?" I asked.

Monday filled me in. "We heard the fire alarm, but it was just in our room. It was so weird. We were sleeping—out cold— so we were totally discombobulated. Didn't think to grab our coats or anything."

"Do you think the guys that made you promise to date them were the ones that played the fire drill noise just outside your door?" Thinking like a guy helped me figure out this puzzle.

I watched as Radia and Monday stared at each other.

"Shit!" Radia started to laugh.

"Those donkeys. How did we not figure that out?" Monday reached over and grabbed my hand.

I laughed with them as they wondered at the dorm guys' deviousness.

I gently rubbed my finger on Monday's hand. I wasn't letting go until she wanted me to. I watched as Radia took in the hand-holding and then passed Monday a not-sneaky-at-all look of appreciation.

We got dessert and another bottle of wine before it was time to wrap it up. Radia was excited to have Monday come to her place for a "sleepover," so after I helped her put her suitcase into Radia's trunk, I gave her a kiss on the cheek.

I headed back to my hotel alone. My *head* head was swimming with her. And the fact that I could have had her was not lost on my balls. If they could give me the middle finger, they would.

I was looking forward to a long shower and some self-satisfaction, but Poncy with the punchable face was leaning against my door, altering all of my plans.

Poncy pushed himself away from my door and stuck his hands into his pockets.

I gave him a man nod and twirled my truck keys on my finger, waiting. I wasn't starting this conversation.

His face had healed. It still looked stupid to me, but there was no bruising that I could see.

"How much?" Poncy pulled a wallet out of his front pocket.

Of all the things he could start with, that had to be the most insulting. "What the hell are you on about?"

Poncy's large Adam's apple bobbed up and down.

"Chestnut told me that you're the issue. That you kissed Monday. I just want to know how much it would take to get you to go away." Poncy stood there like I owed him money and an explanation.

"Pretty sure you broke into her place with her mother's key when you were obviously not supposed to be there." I was feeling violence rise up in me again.

"Is that what she told you? Monday has quite an imagination. Sometimes you just can't believe her." Poncy rocked back on his heels.

"You're going to get out of my way. You can leave the way you came or in an ambulance." I had to hold one fist with my other hand so I wouldn't put this asshole in his place.

Poncy's eyes widened. "Wow. Sorry, bro. I didn't know you were hell-bent on getting in here." He stepped to the side.

"I'm not your bro. Go do something else and stop talking. Especially about Monday." I dug my key card out and waved it in front of the door.

"Ten thousand. Ten thousand dollars to walk away from her." Poncy really didn't know how to take a hint.

I ignored him. As I closed the door, he spoke up just before it slammed, "Twenty thousand!"

I tossed my keys and the key card onto the desk. That was a lot of freaking money. I tried not to picture my dad's face in the hospital and failed.

I couldn't do it, of course. Dad would hate it. I would hate it. Monday was worth everything, and more. I felt ashamed that my brain did the finance math anyway.

If he was shouting twenty grand, chances were, I could get him to fifty grand, all for the simple act of walking away from a beautiful, hot, kind lady.

CHAPTER 25

BEAR

onday was all over my place and I loved it. Even though she was back at her apartment, I could still feel her here.

She was a great distraction from making a decision about Hanning Electric and whether or not I wanted to take on the business once my dad retired.

With her gone, I had to make some real choices. It wasn't fair to make my father wait. If he was finally considering the cushy life with Mom, I wanted him to be able to swing into that as soon as possible. I was half-angry with myself for leaving him on the hook for as long as I had already. Dad needed a stress-free life.

I looked around my apartment, stacked with projects and half-finished dreams. What other options did I have, really?

Instead of worrying, I basked in the glow of having had Monday. After seeing her all that time ago, she had blown my mind. She was a caring, fun lover, and I really, really was looking forward to our next date. This coming weekend was the gala, so that would have to happen first.

Packing for the gala weekend was really all about my tools and equipment and notes. I packed a few all-black outfits and some casual clothes so I could blend in no matter where I had to go. Thursday night was go time, and despite Monday wanting to do a video appearance, she'd begrudgingly agreed to appear for the auction. That meant she was going with me again. Instead of staying with Radia, though, she was bunking in my hotel room.

I made sure to include a nice handful of condoms, even though I knew we would both be busy. When I picked her up at her apartment, she was already waiting in the parking lot. She had a suitcase and a garment bag on a hanger.

"Hey, beautiful. Need a ride?" I hopped out of my truck to get her stuff.

"What kind of ride?" She was flirting and I was down.

"Any kind you want. Your wish is my command, gorgeous." I held her door open, stopping myself from kissing her because of where we were located. I still needed the facade of being on the up and up business wise.

Once we had cleared the parking lot, I took advantage of the first red light to lean over for a kiss.

She wrapped her hand around my head and extended the kiss until after the light turned green. The car behind us honked twice before we separated.

"What are your events this weekend?" I eased onto the highway.

She was holding her phone, checking emails. "According to the schedule Mrs. Nutwell sent out, we have a meet and greet with the bidders before the gala, and we can answer any questions they have there. Then we have the gala itself which will have the auction. Later, we have the after-gala breakfast, but I don't think I want to go to that. What about you?"

I squinted one eye as I tried to visualize my plan. "Well, I have to go over the connections of any light work that was installed this weekend. I want to upload and run the program I designed a few times tonight, just so I can see if there are any bugs or things I missed. Mostly, I'll be working on my own projects while Burnie and the crew handle the outdoor lighting and making sure that the hotel can take the amount of wattage we'll be pulling this weekend. There's always something we miss. I'm just trying to tell the future." I reached over and held her hand. She squeezed mine back.

"That's good. Let me know if you need any help. I brought my portfolio to be shown during the auction. It's the same as all the pictures I sent to you via email, but I have them for backup if we need them." She pulled her hair over her shoulder.

"Better to be safe than sorry. Hopefully, I'll have everything up and running with no problems." I focused on the road. "Do we have a plan for Poncy?"

I'd skirted around the topic in text messages, but I wanted a review in person here.

"Ignore, ignore. I think that's best for my whole family. After the stress of the gala auction is over, I'll investigate mending things with my family. This weekend I made a commitment, and I plan on seeing it through. They know it's my last one. So, as far as I'm concerned, they have the information and I just need to give my spiel and paint a session for someone." She let out a big sigh that made me believe that she still had quite a great deal on her mind. "Thanks for not selling me out to Poncy, by the way,"

"I'm sorry that's a sentence you ever had to say. That man is a jackhole. I'd happily hit him again if you need me to." I flexed my hand into a fist.

"I'll let you know. I can't promise I won't punch him in the mouth when I see him." She also wrapped her hand in a fist.

"Can't damage the assets there." I pointed at her hands with my pinky.

"My boobs?" She pointed at her breasts.

"Well, those, too, but I meant your hands. You need those to do your art and teach your kids." I reached over and covered her fist with my hand. "You interested in the diner for tonight's dinner?"

"Oh, you really enjoyed my old high school haunt." She seemed tickled. "Let's do it."

AFTER WE WERE SITTING in the same booth as last time, I took her hand. "Are you comfortable with this weekend? Do you have any concerns?"

I wanted to know how she was approaching this event. Seeing her family and Poncy's family had to be giving her stress.

She closed her eyes for a few seconds before responding. "Yeah. I don't know. Part of me wants to make a huge scene and make my mother regret everything she's done. And part of me just wants to be done. I mean, she put Poncy above me. It's really going to be hard for her to redeem herself in my eyes." Her eyes filled with tears.

"That's her loss, Monday. You're an amazing daughter." I rubbed my thumbs on her hands. She took one away to use the napkin from the dispenser on the table to dab at her eyes. "I didn't mean to upset you."

She tucked the napkin into her purse and shook her head. "No, it's okay. I really should try to lay out what I expect to happen. I know Mom pretty freaking well."

Our server interrupted to take our meal order. After

repeating our meal from last time, we had the space to talk again.

"I know your auction offering is top billing. They have it listed in the biggest font in the lighted case in the lobby."

"Yeah. They're hitting the 'last one' drum pretty hard. I think they're hoping it will bring more money in." Our server dropped off water and our shakes.

"Will they do it first or last?" I was trying to remember the brochure that I had perused.

"Oh, last. They always make me go last. They hint at it all night."

"Like a surprise superstar."

She gave me a soft smile. "Yeah, just like that."

"So what else will you be required to do?" While monitoring the lights and effects, I fully intended on keeping an eye on Monday as well.

"I'll have to talk up some of the big donors, and I usually take a picture with any previous auction winners that happen to be attending." She stirred her water with the straw.

"And Poncy?" I had no idea what his role was in this event.

"He should keep his distance. Especially if he wants people to think we're still together. If you weren't working, I'd pull you out on the dance floor and out him as a liar." She rolled her eyes.

"Hey, I can get a fifteen-minute break. If you need that, we'll do it." I liked the idea of claiming her in front of all the fancy folk.

"I'll consider it, for sure. Mom would die. Mrs. Nutwell would pass out." She smiled at the thought.

"Seems like a good option then." I tucked into my burger almost as soon as it was set down.

After we finished our meal, I paid and we headed out. "Do you want to go to the hotel and check in? I can drop you off before I get started on running things over at the NBCC."

She put her seatbelt on. "That would make sense. I can take

out my dress and make sure it doesn't need to be steamed. My family will be having their pre-gala fight, as is tradition, so I don't mind missing out on that."

"Okay. Will they actually get in a brawl?" Her family was so different from the way I was raised.

"Not usually. Most of the time there are broken plates and tossed art pieces. Slammed doors. It's rare that they actually come to putting hands on each other. Mom will yell, my father will sulk, and my sisters will rage." Monday seemed tired of it all. Just knowing her like I did now, fighting didn't seem like it was her default setting.

"When will you see them first then?" I wanted to make sure I was close when that happened.

"When I get to the gala tomorrow. My mother will tell me my gown is wrong and my makeup is flat. I'd bet money on it." Monday unbuckled as we pulled into the check-in loop at the hotel.

She leaned over and gave me a lingering kiss. The things I could dream up to do with her in that hotel room flooded my mind. We ended the kiss and I got out to get her bags and mine. After we checked in, I was getting nervous about missing the meeting. I set our belongings on the rolling cart.

"Go. It's okay. I don't want you to be late." She kissed me again and started pushing the cart toward the elevator.

It would be fine. It's a nice hotel. But I couldn't place the sinking feeling that I was getting. I swallowed it and turned my back on her.

CHAPTER 26

MONDAY

*I*t took me a few tries to line the large luggage cart up with the opening on the elevator. When I was inside, I shimmied alongside it to press the third-floor button. I could've sworn the button gave me the tiniest of zaps.

Oh no. Not my old frenemy, electricity. I recognized that it had been nice to me lately. Maybe a little too nice. I hadn't even had any real powerful static electricity jolts this year.

I eyed the illuminated buttons. They flashed once. Then the whole elevator went dark in the blink of an eye. Before I could scream, the lights were back on. After a slow turning of gears, the elevator seemed to want to head back down to the lobby. I hit the number three again.

The elevator ground to a halt and then reversed directions. It delivered me safely to the third floor. I stared at it as I pushed my cart out.

It was a warning. The small scare to remind me who was in charge, who was always in charge. Even if I was dating an electrician. If I could give it a sacrifice to acknowledge that it could make me its bitch whenever it wanted, I would've done so.

Instead, I just used my key card to open up the hotel door.

Things would be fine. The electricity would mind its business, my mother wouldn't tackle scream when she saw me tomorrow, and my painting session would be my last, uneventful experience raising money for the Hartford Greens Country Club.

I was willing this into reality. Manifesting it. I looked around the room and noticed that all the outlets looked like a set of eyes with matching, shocked mouths. There were a lot of them. More than normal? I would say so. Odd heights. Also yes.

Shaking off the feeling that those ever-open O mouths were singing the *Jaws* theme, I unzipped my suitcase and started to unpack. Being distrustful of electricity for sure put me in a tough spot.

After I hung my gala dress in the bathroom, I set the water in the shower to blisteringly hot and closed the door. A good ten minutes in a makeshift steam room would make the wrinkles from travel fall right out. I had a pile of papers to grade for school, so I set them on the desk.

I should have a few hours in a peaceful hotel room to knock out a few grades. Everything was good. Fine. Boring.

BEAR

For some reason, the lights around Monday's advertisement refused to work properly. Every other auction had a little cubby set up in the lobby highlighting what was included in the prize that was up for grabs.

Monday's beautiful face and the lights around her portfolio screen were giving me the business. The iPad that was scrolling through previous winners' portraits flashed on and off, dividing the screen into triangles while it did so. I checked the connections, the code, and the batteries. Nothing seemed out of the ordinary. I bypassed the battery issue using an extension cord to connect the iPad to constant electricity instead of depending on the batteries inside.

After a few more checks, Monday's cubby finally stopped being a problem. This cursed by electricity thing was not something I was too concerned about. But this whole iPad and light debacle was giving me pause. I mean, I believed that Monday thought that electricity had it out for her, but having worked with it for so many years, I found it hard to believe. I think she was just surrounded by incompetent adults that let her down supervision-wise.

The NBCC was super busy as it was turned into a winter wonderland. There were artsy snowmen and my falling snowflakes. Well "falling" snowflakes. I had them light up in a pattern that mimicked tumbling, dancing precipitation.

I made a few more notes and then stashed my tools and equipment where Burnie and his crew had theirs.

"See you in the morning, Bear, bright and early." Burnie gave me a parting handshake.

It was going to be a big day. I didn't see any Nutwells or any of Monday's family. When I mentioned it to her upon arriving back at the hotel room, she was not surprised.

"Oh, today is a huge pre-party day. There will be spa visits and colonics, fasting and cold sculpting. A little Botox, too."

Her black dress was hanging on the closet door and she had on leggings and a tank top.

"Did you finish grading your papers?" I started peeling off

my clothes. I wanted to grab a quick shower before I grabbed her.

"Yes. I got that done. What time do you have to leave in the morning?" She stood and leaned against the doorframe like I was putting on a show.

"I have to be at the job site by five-thirty. It's going to be a long day." I unbuckled my belt and slid the leather off.

Monday bit her knuckle while she watched.

"Everything okay?" I set the belt down on the chair.

"No problem at all." She tilted her head.

"Mind if I grab a shower?" I thumbed over my shoulder toward the bathroom.

"Mind if I join you in a few?" She pointed in the direction I was planning on heading.

"That would be my pleasure. And yours." I dropped my pants and headed to get the water started.

I opened the glass door and slid in. Once I was clean, Monday's silhouette appeared on the other side of the steamy shower door.

I pushed on it to open it up. Monday had a chill as she stepped in and I grabbed her hips to steady her. "Careful, the tile's slippery."

Shower sex was dangerous and seemed like it would be great but ultimately resulted in bruises and pulled tendons, but shower foreplay? That made a man believe in miracles.

Seeing her soaped up and in the full light was what daydreams were made of. My male brain growled in approval. I wanted to touch all of her soft skin at once. My hands were greedy, grabbing a handful of breasts and then wanting to slip farther south. Once Monday was almost useless, I reached over and turned off the water. The orgasm I was planning on giving her needed to have a sturdy, safe place to lay her down.

After she swayed at the loss of my touch, I offered her my hand. Instead, she grabbed my erection. "Lead the way."

In a clumsy shuffle, I got her to one of the two queen beds. "The sex bed." I lifted her by her hips and tossed her gently onto the mattress.

She laughed as she bounced, her wet hair plastering itself on her chest like a scrolling design. I ran my hand from her hip to her knee, watching her leave her inhibitions behind. She let her legs fall open and I died.

This gorgeous woman, revealing her most sensitive places to me, hit me hard. I touched myself while she did the same. When her hand started moving too aggressively for my liking, I nuzzled my way between her legs. She started moving counter-clockwise underneath me, and at first I was confused, but then I got it. Monday used the leverage of the bed to get her mouth around my dick while I had my mouth on her.

And then we were battling to stay focused on our task while the other person used all the skills they had.

We were as close to simultaneous orgasm as two humans could be. When I fell, I made sure to go to my side so I wouldn't crush her. I shifted so that both of our heads were hanging off the end of the bed.

We were both panting and grinning.

Monday was the first to talk. "That was the dirtiest shower ever."

I slid my bicep under her head as a pillow. "That was spectacular. Are you starving? I'm starving."

She nodded. After we could both sit, I ordered us breakfast foods. Pancakes, eggs, and bacon seemed like a brilliant idea right about now.

Monday disappeared into the bathroom and returned with two fuzzy white robes. After I helped her put hers on, she helped me tie the knot on mine. We cuddled on the sex bed while we waited to eat.

"I think your man stick is even better than the one I painted on you back in the day." Monday outlined said body part with her index finger.

"So glad it doesn't disappoint. I have to say, the picture was something to live up to, for sure." I matched her tracing around her left breast and was rewarded with her nipple peaking under my touch. Before we could get ourselves all hot and bothered again, the room service server was knocking on the door.

I hopped up and opened the door as Monday cuddled under the blankets.

A tall man wheeled in the service cart and lifted the cloches with panache. "Breakfast for the lovebirds."

I passed him a ten-dollar bill and escorted him out of the room. The smell of the food lured Monday out from the bed, and I took the serving dishes and plates to the table in our room. We had a few very domestic moments where we set the table together before sitting down.

"This is great. Perfect idea. I feel so wiped all of a sudden." She rubbed her eyes.

I could feel my melatonin levels rising, because sleep was calling to me as well. We ate our fill and left all the plates and food right on the table.

After a quick speed hump, we both cuddled naked in bed.

Five-thirty in the morning came quickly and the darkness was still hanging on to the sky.

CHAPTER 27

MONDAY

*W*hen I heard my alarm, Bear was long gone. Even though I had the early wake-up time of seven-thirty, he had already been at work for hours. I took a few seconds to gloat in my head about my sexy night. My toes curled thinking of all the different ways Bear knew how to use his fingers.

I had to take another shower and get ready for the day. There would be a few news reporters at the event this morning, and me talking up the painting session would be expected.

I had to put on my outfit and apply my makeup in a way that it would stay on all day. Lots of waterproof and long-lasting formulas later, I was ready to leave. I glanced at my phone as I stuck it in my purse. The battery was low enough to make me concerned, and there were notifications for a lot of text messages.

First and last were both from Bear. He missed me, he

couldn't stop thinking about last night, and he hoped we could do some similar things tonight.

I agreed with all of those assessments, so I emphasized the comments with a heart. Also, there were tons of texts from Mrs. Nutwell and a fistful from my mother as well. None from Poncy, so I was taking that as a win.

I checked my outfit one last time in the full-length mirror. The black dress was formfitting and strapless. The bottom had a touch of flare. My hair was long and loose, and I had simple gold jewelry on. I fastened my high heels on last, wanting to give my feet their best chance of surviving the long day.

I had all the things I needed and I grabbed my key card last. It wasn't until I was in the lobby that I realized the day was overcast and windy. I went to the taxi stand and ordered a car service. A black Escalade pulled up and the license plate matched the one listed on the app.

After slipping into the back seat, the driver spoke up, "Let me guess, the Hartford Greens Gala?" He tilted his rearview mirror so I could make eye contact.

"Yes, please. How'd you know?" I clipped my seatbelt in place.

"Oh, you're my third ride over there today. I have a feeling I'll be going back and forth there all day." He put his blinker on and eased into traffic.

The wind picked up again, and a giant branch came down alongside the car.

"This weather is only supposed to get worse. Do you have an umbrella with you?" He kept his eyes on the traffic light.

"No, I didn't even bring one from home." I peered at the dark gray clouds that swiftly moved through the sky. Rain would do a number on my hair.

"I'll call ahead and ask one of the valets to make sure they have one for you." The driver made that exact call on his steering wheel. I knew this guy was getting a five-star review for sure.

When we arrived, the rain had just started to pick up, so the valet with the golf umbrella was a welcome sight. I waved goodbye to my driver and the young, tall valet made sure I was completely covered from the rain until we were under the awning.

"Thank you so much. I would've hated to do my hair again with the hand dryers in the bathroom." He nodded at me but seemed preoccupied. I imagined adding rain and tons of fancy dressed people to his day made everything that much more complicated.

Once in the lobby, Mrs. Nutwell flagged me down. "Here she is now. Our prized show horse, if you will. Monday Blue, this is *Living New Lives Magazine* reporter Jonathan Pipes. He's going to be live at the event and he has some questions for you."

I smiled at Jonathon even though Mrs. Nutwell had a strong grip on my upper arm. She hiss-whispered in my ear, "Nothing out of the ordinary. We just want to raise money, right?"

I pulled hard until my arm was free. I didn't dignify her with an answer. Jonathan stood and held out a hand to shake.

"Lovely to meet you, Monday. I have to say you've been the buzz here for the last week. Everyone is very excited to bid on the last ever Monday Blue session for auction." He flipped open his notebook and poised his pen.

"That's great to hear." I motioned to the chair set he seemed to want to do our interview in. He nodded and waited for me to sit.

Once I was settled, he also set up a voice recorder. "Is this okay? Sometimes I get so caught up I forget to take notes. This keeps me honest." Jonathan had very white teeth and it seemed like he used every one of them to smile at me.

"No problem. I want to make sure you get what you need."

He pressed the buttons to start the tape running. "So first things first, when's the date for you and Poncy Nutwell?"

I looked over my shoulder to see Mrs. Nutwell's eyes on me. She would for sure hear my answer from where she was standing, which I realized was by design.

"No date." I tried to smile. That was the best I was going to do.

"Well, that's very exciting. Maybe I can cover that as well?" Jonathan tapped his pencil against the paper.

I gave him a noncommittal smile. He'd have a great human-interest story if I told him the truth: that I had dumped Poncy hard and had no intention of getting involved with his family.

"So, I researched your previous sessions and last year was the record-breaking sale. Do we anticipate this sale taking the new crown?" Jonathan crossed his legs.

"I hope so. I'd love to raise as much money to help as we can. And I want the auction winner to be happy with their purchase." I tucked my left hand under my right. I didn't have a ring on, obviously. It didn't feel great smooshing the truth around like play dough. Jonathan seemed like a very well-versed journalist. I wondered how well he could tell if someone was lying because I was pretty sure I had all of the warning signals popping off. I wasn't even close to being engaged.

Our conversation held a few more low intensity questions, and then I was up and moving to another table that had a placard for a different magazine. I answered similar versions of the same question two or three times when I was done with the press junket. There was a huge emphasis on the fact that this would be my last auction. It seemed like the Nutwells were planning on taking me out back and putting me out of my misery after the gala.

All at once, as I was standing, the power went out in the hotel. We were all plunged into darkness.

There were a few yells and a few swears. Soon enough, everyone had the flashlights on their cell phones open and shedding light on the large room. Once every minute or so, lightning flared outside. The room was so dark, so quickly. The hairs at the nape of my neck stood up. This room felt like it was inside one of those crazy plasma balls they use at science museums. It occurred to me that there was a real overabundance of windows.

Easy to see the show Mother Nature was putting on.

I texted Bear.

You okay?

Yes. You?

I'm good. Is this in your wheelhouse?

I didn't get a response, so I imagined the answer was yes. I felt a hand come around my waist. I turned, expecting to see Bear, but instead, it was Poncy.

"You've been avoiding my calls." Poncy somehow made his chin stick out farther in the beam of my cell phone flashlight.

"You've been bothering my phone." I stepped away from his hand, but his fingers dug into my hip.

"Stay here. The journalists are watching." He gave me a smile that didn't reach his eyes.

"Honestly, what do I owe you? I don't care if the journalists are looking." I covered his hand with mine and began the process of peeling his fingers open.

"Did you know your mom was caught stealing products from the swag bags?" He leaned closer to me like he was telling me a joke.

"What? What are you even talking about?" This was business Poncy. He was in what he referred to as "shark mode." I recognized it from when he would brag about closing a deal because he was such a great businessman.

"Chestnut wanted the expensive lipstick out of quite a few of them. My mother said that security had to have her empty her pockets. Very sad to see." Poncy made a pouty face, like I might be inclined to kiss him.

The lights flickered on and off, and then the lightning flashed over and over. Combining it with the thunder was nerve rattling for anyone, never mind a lady with a history with the beast.

"Let go of me, Poncy, or I'll scream." I pointed at his hand. There might even be some bruising where he'd been hanging on to me.

He let go with one hand but snatched my wrist with his other hand. "I suggest you stay here and have a nice evening with me. Then we won't have to press charges against your mother."

The lights flashed again, and I happened to lock gazes with the woman in question. Mom looked nervous, but she didn't look guilty. It wasn't sitting right with me. My mother loved to spend money. Loved thinking about spending money. Wanted people to see her spend money. It didn't connect with me that Mom would dip into the free swag.

Poncy put his arm around my shoulders and Mom crossed the space just as a set of dim lights came up. I heard someone mumble about the backup generator, which was what I was guessing was giving us the light we now had.

When my mother finally reached me, she had a look of concern on her face.

"You okay, Monday? I know you hate these kinds of storms." She put one hand out and then seemed to think better of it and let it fall to her side.

In that moment I saw a glimpse of the mom that actually had feelings for me, no matter how much horrible judgment she implemented on my behalf.

"Poncy won't get off of me. And I'd rather be standing outside under a giant metal pole than have him touch me." I picked up his hand and tossed it off my shoulder.

162

Mom, to her credit, put herself between Poncy and me to give us some distance. "Quarrels are part of life. Sometimes we need a breather from each other."

After watching Mom mouth something to Poncy, she pulled me behind her, leaving him standing alone.

When we got to the other side of the event, I noticed she had dragged me to where my father and sisters were.

"Monday, are you okay?" My father startled as a large clap of thunder made us all feel like we were in a shooting range. As targets.

I nodded. Their base level concern for my well-being humbled me a bit. I was mad. I had every right to be mad, but these people were my family and I felt myself weakening in my hardline stance of never wanting to speak to them again.

Brent, Lottie's man, came close, all decked out in his tuxedo. "Hey, Monday, you clean up nice."

He held up his fist and my job was to bump it. I did it and he shuffled near my sister.

I stepped closer to my mother. "Did you take lipstick out of the swag bags?"

I needed to know if there was any truth to what Poncy had said.

The indignant expression on her face spoke to her innocence. "Who told you that?"

"Who do you think?" I hiked my thumb over my shoulder.

Mother's mouth opened in surprise and then snapped closed at the exact moment a bolt of lightning sizzled through the room.

"Hit the deck!" Father used his massive dad instincts to push all four women around him to the floor.

I went to my knees as he pulled us forward to protect us with his body.

Two more bolts of lightning snaked into the event space, popping off on various chandeliers. More screaming ensued as the backup generator failed and we were once again in the dark.

I glanced around the room when it flashed to extreme brightness. Many of the workers, press, and photographers were splayed out on the floor. I reached down and pulled on the top of my dress. It was not made for these kinds of quick movements.

"Freaking Monday, this is the shit that happens when you are around." Lottie spat out in my direction.

She would blame me. Hell, honestly, I blamed me. Like a jump scare in a horror movie, someone grabbed my ankle just as I was about to start fighting with my sister. I whipped around to see Poncy holding on to me.

Lottie turned her ire to my feet. "Poncy Nutwell, so help me, if you don't let go of my sister, I will donkey kick you in the butthole."

He released my ankle and had the sense to look ashamed. I turned back to my sister in surprise.

"What? I can be mad at you, but he can't grab you," my sister huffed.

If I wasn't so busy crawl/rolling away from Poncy, I'd have given my sister a tiny smile. She was a pain in my ass, but she also didn't want anyone else taking that job away from her.

Stupid family. They got on my last nerve for some very valid reasons, but my sister's reaction to Poncy made me think their support of him might not be as full-throated as I thought.

The wind picked up outside. It almost sounded like a train or a herd of trains headed right for us. The pressure in the room dropped tremendously. This was it. I wasn't sure what "it" was, but it had the makings of something horribly wrong.

BEAR

If it could go wrong, it was going wrong. At no point did we consider three different types of storms spinning up on top of the event space the day of the gala. Sure, I had plans for inclement weather, but I had not sketched out what to do in an apocalypse.

A reporter was delivering his spiel to the camera, using me working on the fuse box as his backdrop.

"Today we are witnessing a very rare weather event. The wild drop in temperature, along with the blistering humidity, has kicked up a three-part storm that is as vicious as it is sudden." He gestured to me and then the window beyond me. I legitimately would not be surprised if the Wicked Witch of the West went flying by in the swirling rain and wind.

"The bomb cyclone, combined with the record-topping winds, has us all on flood and tornado watch. As you well know, Elise, these kinds of weather events have been becoming more violent and spontaneous." He whirled back to the camera and I tried to bury my face in my work. "I'm Jonathan Pipes, and I'll cover every second of this event. Back to you, Elise." The reporter relaxed his arm with the microphone in it. "We good? Got it?"

The cameraman nodded. "They said they can cut back to you the second we want them to, but it better be worth it if we do."

Jonathan rolled his eyes. "Here we are risking our lives. They know it'll damn well be worth it." He crossed over the cameraman and seemed to be checking the footage.

The panel was good. I left it open just because it would save me a few seconds if I needed to get to any specific fuse.

I checked the local electric company's website, and they didn't have any outages listed yet. So either we were too new at the outage or something was wrong with the wiring and the electric company would not know that the power here was down. While I was deciding which one of those two options was the reality, Burnie came up next to me.

"We are secure outside—as best we can be. That room has way too many windows, and Burt just told me that there was a possible tornado sighting a few miles away." Burnie pointed at the offending glass.

It had to be the worst room in the history of man to choose to be in during a tornado. I stepped around Burnie and set out to find Monday. There was no way in hell I was leaving her to face this by herself. The lightning was so frequent, she had to feel like the bolts were spelling out her name.

Burnie kept speed with me. "I think if we get them into the hallways, that might be the best bet."

Why this was our job, I wasn't sure. But being electricians, we knew how to keep a level head in sticky situations. I looked for Monday's hair in combination with her black dress. A lot of women could have played her stunt double in the movie that could be made of this evening. But eventually, it was stupid Poncy that made her stand out. He was sitting up and frowning like a spoiled child. After taking big, leaping steps, I made it to her. Poncy seemed to want to touch her or at the very least be next to her. I stepped over his legs and squatted down next to Monday, making sure my butt was sticking in Poncy's face.

She wrapped her arms around me and gave me a full kiss on the mouth. Her pulse was hammering away like a fox running from a herd of hound dogs.

"This sucks. Are you okay?" She put her hand on my cheek and then ran it through my hair.

"I'm good. We have to move everyone somewhere else. There are too many windows here." I tried to guess how many people we had in the room altogether.

It was hard. People were hiding under tables that had long tablecloths on them. Even more were being directed into the hall from the outdoors. They were drenched, obviously encountering the harsh weather on their way into the event from their cars. It was far from a fancy red carpet entry now.

I hunched down as I led Monday to the hallway. When I turned around, I noticed she had dragged her mother with her, who had a train of people behind her.

And I knew Monday had had it with her family, but I loved that at this moment, she wasn't leaving them out.

We picked our way through the hallway until I found a sturdy looking alcove. Monday held my elbow as her family tucked themselves into the safe space. Even dumbass Poncy was here.

"Do you have to go?" Monday searched my face as she waited for her answer.

"Yeah. We're going to try to get everyone out of that room. It's going to be crowded here." I kissed her forehead and I heard Poncy snort like an old pug dog falling back asleep in his bed.

I turned toward him and pointed a finger in his face. "I will literally hand you your asshole like a present if you so much as look at her."

Poncy tried to look everywhere but at me. Monday gave my elbow a squeeze. "Be safe. And you're a contractor, don't get too involved. Come back soon." She smelled beautiful, which was a stupid thing to notice, but it was a fact.

When I made it back to the window room, Burnie had started encouraging the guests into a line, headed to the hallway.

A manager paced in front of the doors. "We have a maintenance level and also a wine cellar. Though being surrounded by glass bottles may be a poor choice," she spoke into an earpiece and went pale.

"What's up?" I tilted my head toward her.

"They think the tornado is two blocks away." She pulled out her phone and started texting.

I hustled around her and stood near Burnie. "We don't have a lot of time."

After seeing him look around, worried, I put my fingers in my mouth and whistled like I was calling a herd of cattle home. "Go! Go! Go!"

I started waving my hand to spur some urgency. The women were dressed to the nines and teetering on high heels.

We could hear the wind getting impossibly louder. I used the stopper to prop the door open wider.

The people were damn near moseying. Burnie took a cue from me, and we started being more aggressive and urgent in our movements.

I saw Monday duck back into the ballroom and thread her way across the room.

"Monday!" I sidestepped some of the people to follow her.

Now that the weather was so audible, I didn't have to make the urgency known. I could feel the change of weather in my chest, and I was betting a lot of other people could feel it, too.

She didn't slow down but ducked into the ladies' room.

It was a horrible idea to come back into this room to use the restroom. The floor-to-ceiling glass windows were just begging to shatter.

I banged on the door when I got there. After I had no response, I pushed the door in. "Monday?"

She was in the middle of wrangling an older woman in a power wheelchair.

"Oh, good. Please help. A friend told me that she had seen this woman in here, and I said I'd check on her. She's out of charge on the wheelchair battery."

The woman was dressed in a silver dress and looked scared out of her mind. "I thought I was going to be left." She dabbed at her eyes with a small wad of tissue.

"No, ma'am." Monday comforted her.

The wild wind kicked up even more. I hated that we were all so far from the hallway. I leaned over. "Okay, hang on. We're getting moving."

Carrying her was the only option. I tried to be careful because the older woman felt frail, but we also needed to move. Monday held the door for me and my new burden.

After I was out, she came right behind me. I made a beeline straight for the doors that Burnie was in the midst of trying to close.

"Hey! We're coming through!" I yelled like there was a tornado bearing down on us and that caught his attention. His eyes went wide and looked over my shoulder.

I held the older woman with one arm and reached behind me. Monday clasped my wrist as I whipped her around me and through the door. As soon as I cleared the door, I set the woman down against the wall. I'd keep track of her.

I turned to help Burnie secure the doors and saw what had been brewing behind me. A generous, deep, gray-green tornado was teetering its way straight at us. We slammed the doors closed and one of the other guys slid a metal broom through the door handles. The dark was complete now, except for the flickers of lightning that found its way through various smaller windows.

I gathered Monday in my arms and we both slid down next to the older woman. Burnie took shelter on the other side of us.

I tried racking my brain, thinking about the fact that the huge room seemed empty. The breaking glass just beyond the door sounded like Godzilla kickboxing the windows. There were some screams and we waited to see what the tornado had in store for us.

Monday burrowed her face in my chest, and I wrapped my arms around her hard. In my head I was trying to imagine the things we would have to do if the tornado breached the ball-room and came into the hallway.

There were few places we could go. Things were not looking good.

CHAPTER 28

MONDAY

$\mathcal{T}$he fact that we were huddling scared with a tornado raging outside was extraordinary. We never got this type of weather. From my place in Bear's strong arms, I peered at the older woman. I had concerns that our fast escape had injured her ribs because she couldn't stop holding them.

The vortex had to be over us. I could almost feel the air getting sucked out of my lungs while the ceiling groaned. I glanced up and the roof lifted just enough for me to see the chaos beyond, way above us.

I flinched as things started hitting the roof and the building.

It occurred to me that nature doesn't have a sound limit. Things were going to be as loud as they were, whether it was too loud for my ears or not. It felt like we would be at war with the gods forever, and then, like the snap of a finger, it was done.

As we picked ourselves up off the floor, we hoped everyone was uninjured.

"How are you?" I checked the older woman Bear had carried.

"Good. My son is here now." She patted the arm of the man next to her.

Bear was already in the hallway, asking people how they were. There were some cuts and bruises, but miraculously nothing to be concerned about.

My mother, Poncy, and my sisters were fine as well. I saw my father and he nodded at me. They had all made me angry but being able to see them safe was a comfort.

Bear stepped toward the door that normally led into the ballroom, and when he pulled it open, there was a distinct lack. A lack of a barrier. He ran his hand over his hair and rubbed it back and forth. I clambered next to him and then marveled. The ballroom was just...gone.

There were no fancy tables, no tablecloths, nothing. The tornado had taken them. Sure, there were smashed bits of things that used to have a purpose, but now it was just rubble.

While I was still processing, Bear turned and cupped his hands around his mouth. "Burnie! Ask around and see if anyone is missing!"

As I saw the roadway just beyond the NBCC, I shivered. I couldn't imagine having to ride out the storm in a room that was erased so thoroughly. Surely they wouldn't have made it. The noise alone would be a game changer.

Burnie mimicked Bear's motion and put his hands around his mouth as well. "We're all accounted for down here!"

I watched as Bear's shoulders slumped in relief. He was one of the good ones. The fact that he could only relax when he knew everyone was safe was a character definer. He was next level as a person. I told him so and kissed him on the cheek. He kept his arm around my waist as we picked through the debris.

"What does this mean for you? I mean, the electricity is out as far as I can tell. And the destruction speaks for itself. I'm assuming the auction will be held at a later date."

Bear surveyed the damage. "It's going to have to be. I can't even begin to list the problems that they will have here returning this place back to its former glory."

As we moved around the space, and everyone was accounted for, emergency personnel showed up.

Checking phones and news sources, we found that the tornado hit us as if it targeted us. Only a few miles north and south of NBCC were destroyed, and most of it through the woods.

Police came through with flashlights. "If you have a vehicle here, and it's operational, we are going to ask you to move out."

My mother came close to me, then she pulled me into a hard hug. "I'm so glad we're okay."

I hugged her back. The tornado had taken us down to a primal level. Instead of a fancy event with fancy problems, we were just making sure we were still on the planet.

My sisters joined in the hug, and soon my father was near, patting our backs.

I stepped away as Poncy approached. "I'm going to see if Bear needs help."

We still had crap to deal with regarding Poncy and this whole show, but I was happy they were okay.

Bear and Burnie were in a conversation with the manager, and I came close to them.

Burnie was shaking his head. "There's nothing we can do right now safely. We have to wait until the power company has cleared us to do work. They're going to be swamped for days, if not weeks."

Bear pointed at the empty ballroom. "We have to see how far the devastation goes. First, I think we need to evacuate everyone here. If you have a contact that can get buses in here, that would be my recommendation. And speak to the fire chief. They just arrived."

The manager thanked them for their input, and then Bear turned to me. "The hotel is still standing. As soon as we make sure the woman from the bathroom is okay, I think maybe we should drive your family out of here and then head back to the hotel."

"Is your truck okay?" I felt disoriented. I knew where he had parked before, but I had no idea if that was an accessible thing to achieve.

"I saw a glimpse of it from the new open-air ballroom. I'll double-check." He put his hand on my shoulder and gave me a kiss on top of the head.

While he went to survey our options, I made it back to my parents, who were huddled together, looking stunned.

"Bear can give you all a lift out of here if you need it and if his truck can roll out." I spoke mostly to my father, but my sisters were paying attention.

I watched my father and mother exchange a glance. They seemed to speak without talking. However they had arrived, that was clearly not an option anymore.

And that's how I wound up packing my parents and family into the back of Bear's work truck. It was really satisfying to lock the doors on them after they were all sitting on the floor.

"Any chance you can take the turns on two wheels a few times?"

Bear put his arm around me. "If there's another tornado, I sure as hell will."

He came to my side of the truck and opened the door, offering his hand. When we were both in the cab, we took a second to survey the damage. The sky was now revealing blue skies and sun. It was crazy how quickly the storm had moved on. There were three huge trees down in front of the parking lot and the valet chalet was crumbled under a streetlight.

Bear was able to cruise us out, swerving to avoid obstacles like downed branches and random debris. He did it slowly and carefully.

"I don't want to have anything cut loose in there on your

family."

He pushed the sleeves up on his black shirt, revealing his tattoos. I helped him navigate the landscape to get to my parents' place.

"Wow. This is...huge." Bear leaned forward to take in the whole house.

"It was never big enough for my mom." I shook my head.

Bear and I hopped out after he came to a stop. He opened the doors.

My family was doing just fine. Bear held out his hand to the women as they stepped out. He pretty much lifted my mother down completely.

My sisters and their husbands gave a half-hearted thanks and then it was just my parents, Bear, and me in the driveway.

"How'd it look out there?" My father put his hands in his pockets and did the rocking back on his heels thing dads liked to do.

"Spotty. This was for sure a hit-or-miss storm." And with that, my father stepped forward and started quizzing Bear in a respectful way about his opinion of the damage.

Sometimes men were easy. My mother and I looked at each other. Her hair was slightly askew and I reached forward and smoothed it out.

"Oh, thank you." She tilted her head toward her shoulder and then offered an olive branch. Well, the best one she could think of. "You look lovely in that dress."

"Why'd you side with Poncy mom?" And all at once I wanted answers. Being in such a dire situation and seeing fear so close made me want to have a real discussion.

She put her hand on her chest and made wide eyes. "Monday Blue! This is not the time or place for a discussion like that!"

I gestured around widely. "Alone? In your driveway? Is there a special place you want to discuss stabbing your daughter in the back? Is there mood music for that?" Bear and my father's conversation tapered off. I knew what my mother would say before she even got her mouth around the words, so I said them for her, "A woman doesn't raise her voice!"

My mother gently echoed that statement.

"Now is where and when we are having it, Mom. Tell me how you could pick Poncy over me?" I folded my arms in front of my chest.

Mom opened and shut her mouth and then waved her hand around a little. It was like she was trying to find a way out of having to answer, until finally she spoke the truth.

"I really wanted a Nutwell wedding to happen."

Her statement laid in front of us all like a dead snake.

"Okay. Well, thanks for all that. When Poncy is finally married, I hope you get invited. Because you won't be invited to anything I do anymore." I started to pace. "I knew it. I knew it the whole time I was growing up. Money and status meant more than I did. Well done, Chestnut. Great job making me feel like less." I stepped toward Bear who held out his hand. The empathy in his face made my eyes water. I didn't want to cry. I knew all this information, but I guess there was always a part of me that wanted my parents to put me first.

"Wait. Wait a minute." My father held up both of his hands.

And now I was ready for a Dad lecture. He hated to see division in the family and had my sisters and me keep peace with our mother just for the pure ease of the situation for him. He could tell kids how to behave, but now, I was an adult.

Bear put his arm around me and I hugged his middle. This was my guy, with his electric truck that had brought my family to their giant mansion. I was so proud of him. And of me. We'd done everything we could during the tornado.

"Now, your mother would never say Poncy is more important than you." Dad seemed to be starting a lecture. When we were kids, we had to stay quiet and listen. Not anymore.

"She did. More than once. She gave him the key to my place.

She invited him here for dinner." I tipped my chin up in defiance.

It was a moment in my life when I watched my father shift from his role as a father to a man, just another guy—like every other person. He had no right to say what I did or thought anymore.

I watched as his eyes seemed to say goodbye to the little girl he used to tuck into bed at night. I watched his Adam's apple bob up and down as he reassessed.

"Okay. Okay, I hear you. That was in no way okay. Chestnut, really?" He turned to Mom.

I wondered if he only knew part of it. Part of how devious Mom had been. Maybe he just hadn't processed it from my point of view. I could imagine that, for sure.

"Well, she has a responsibility..." Mom trailed off. The look on my father's face of pure disappointment must have stopped her cold.

Bear finished her statement, "...to be happy."

My father and mother whipped their heads in his direction. Bear squeezed me a little tighter.

My father stepped next to my mother and put his arm around her. "Monday, Bear, if you would excuse us? Your mother and I need to have a conversation in private. Thank you so much for the ride home, and I am very glad you're both safe and well."

Dad held out a hand to Bear, who shook it. My mother dabbed at her eyes but didn't meet mine.

My father nodded at me. "I'll call you soon."

And then he and Mom turned and walked the rest of the way up the driveway.

Bear kissed the top of my head and then my forehead. "You okay?"

I shook my head no. I wasn't okay. I started to cry right then and there.

177

CHAPTER 29

BEAR

*a*fter I got Monday settled in her seat, I headed back to the hotel carefully. I got a text from Burnie at a stoplight that we were all dismissed for the current time. Because there was so much cleanup, it could be over a year before the Nutwell Blissful Convention Center was party ready.

I held Monday's hand anytime I could as we drove. I needed to get back to the NBCC to see if I could salvage any of my extra equipment, but for right now, I had a sweet lady with a broken heart.

After parking the truck, we got out at the hotel. It had a few downed branches but didn't have anything that looked like the worst of the damage we had seen from the tornado.

When we walked by the main desk, the attendant's attention was on the news. Live video was being broadcast from around the region. I saw the event space in the split screen. Monday and I got on the elevator and went to our room. She stripped off her dress and crawled into the bed in her Spanx.

She probably didn't consider them sex clothes, but they were hot as hell.

I shucked off my shoes and pulled off my shirt. I was pretty sure Monday needed a good, strong cuddle. I climbed onto the bed and pulled her back to nestle against my chest.

She sighed and wiggled her butt a little at the contact.

"I'm sorry, sunshine." I couldn't imagine the way she had to interact with her family. It had to take a lot out of her. Not having a strong foundation was a horrible way to come into adulthood. "You're a spectacular person, just know that."

She flipped over and then sat up, so I shifted so my back was against the headboard.

"I'm just so angry. I shouldn't have to fight for her approval with a man that is a garbage dump. She feels like the Nutwells are the be-all and end-all of everything. What about me? All I am is related to her, so I guess that makes me a nonentity. What does that say about her? Your crotch fruit is not worthy unless we crawl up some social ladder? I'm sorry." She took a huge breath and I opened my arms. As soon as she lay on my chest, I felt her rigid body go lax.

"I think anger is totally appropriate. I think it's your parents' turn to listen to your expectations for them and not the other way around." I rubbed her back.

Monday was quiet for a little while. And then, "You're wise. You're an electric magician and you're wise. And brave."

"Well, I don't know about all that, but I do take things one step at a time. I learned that from electricity. If you do the steps in the right order, electricity always does the right thing. People? They're not that reliable."

She tucked her leg between mine. I was trying to ignore how much my body loved having hers pressed against mine.

"This has been the most insane day." She hugged me hard.

"Yeah. This was no walk in the park. First, the natural disaster, and then the family confrontation. I do think it was time for you to speak your mind. I think, at least as far as I could tell, it seemed like your father heard you. And your mother got some truth on her." I rubbed my middle finger in small circles on her lower back.

Our conversation tapered off, and soon, Monday was asleep on my chest, and I wasn't going to move for anything.

When we woke hours later, it was because my stomach was rumbling loud enough to make us laugh.

Monday's fancy hair was a mess and one of her eyes had mascara dripping a little. She was beautiful. I used the remote to order us room service. Two waffle meals were ready just as Monday emerged in a sweatshirt and leggings.

I hopped up and paid the tip. The food smelled amazing as Monday and I were eating standing up. By the time we were laughing at each other, I had demolished an entire waffle.

"Let's take the rest of this to the table." She and I moved the trays to the small table.

Food seemed to cheer up Monday. I watched her as she scrutinized her phone.

"Anything?" I took a bite of bacon.

"Dad tried calling a few times. I have him set to go straight to voicemail." She set the phone screen side down. "I'll look at it soon."

It was understandable. She needed a few minutes to wrap her head around the family drama.

My phone rang, and I excused myself to the hall to take it.

"Son? Everything going okay?" My father.

I wouldn't ever take hearing his voice for granted again. The heart attack really put my priorities in a very specific place.

"Yeah, Burnie told me he spoke to you." I leaned against the wall in the hallway.

"He did. Crazy thing. So glad you and your lady friend are okay. Just wanted to make sure that I couldn't do anything to help."

I heard it then—the get up and go that made my dad great at his job. He loved helping people. And a lot of times, he was dealing with people who needed help in this profession.

"Honestly, it's a giant nightmare up here. I mean, the cleanup alone will probably take a year."

"Your mother and I were watching the news. Horrible. So glad no one was hurt as far as they can tell."

"I never understood how complete a tornado could be. I have a greater respect for people who live in the part of the country that has tornadoes in their weather forecast on the regular."

"Yeah. Agreed. Well, you drive home safe and watch for debris and all that."

"You got it, Dad. Thanks, love you."

"Love you, Bear."

That was another thing I'd never take for granted anymore. I wanted my father to hear that I loved him as often as I could.

Burnie rang through right after Dad, so I took his call as well. "We're just packing up here. I've got a laptop that I think is yours, but they are locking down this site. Too dangerous. I'll drive by and drop it off for you."

"That's great. I can come to where you are and pick it up, if you need. You must be tired after going all this time." I glanced at the time on my phone. I hoped Burnie had been home and had a nap, but his voice sounded exhausted, so I was guessing maybe not.

"You know what? If you wouldn't mind. I'm going to head back to the store to return a few things. I could meet you there in fifteen minutes?"

"Will do. See you there." Burnie's shop was just a few blocks away from the hotel, so I walked back into the room to tell Monday I had to go out for a few minutes.

She was on a FaceTime call with her sister.

"I'm not coming to the house. Sorry."

Her sister shuffled the phone, and I briefly got a great look up her nose. "It's an intervention for Mom. She's having an episode."

"Her episodes are carefully orchestrated temper tantrums, and I'm not in the headspace to deal with her dramatics today." Monday moved the phone down so she could roll her eyes at me.

I pulled out my phone and sent her a text so I wouldn't interrupt her conversation.

Got to grab my laptop from Burnie. You okay to stay here, or do you want to come with?

Monday grabbed a pen and paper off the nightstand and scribbled a note.

You go. This is going to be a while.

I had a feeling the trip to Burnie's had something to do with more than my laptop. I hated leaving Monday with her angry virtual sister, but at least I knew she could lock the hotel door and no one could bother her here if she didn't want to be bothered.

I slipped into jeans and a t-shirt and popped a baseball hat on my head. She blew me a kiss and I headed out. It was still nice outside. The night was clear. I never would have imagined so much could change so quickly. The tornado was setting the tone for the day.

CHAPTER 30

MONDAY

*T*he FaceTime call between my sister and me was not a private affair. Mrs. Nutwell appeared behind Teva in the living room of my parents' house as Bear closed the door.

I pointed at the woman and then gave my sister a death glare.

"What? Her? They're here with an emergency board meeting about the auction. You should probably be here, actually." My sister gave me the death glare right back and then she panned the camera around the room.

When she was back in focus, I gave her instructions. "Well, set the phone up and I'll listen, but I'm not coming back to the house. I'm also already in sweats." I touched the front of my shirt.

"Fine. But I can't be without my phone all damn day letting you be on it to attend meetings." My sister made duck lips at me.

"Then don't put me down. Ask me how much I care. It was a

freaking tornado. The last thing anyone should be worrying about is the auction." I slouched back on the bed and held the phone above me.

"I'm doing you a favor here. Seriously, Monday, be a little grateful."

I didn't bring up that I donated my time and skill to the auction. That my sister setting up her phone for a meeting for me wasn't exactly a reason to give her a Nobel Prize.

The phone was adjusted on a table, and the camera was almost eye height with Mrs. Nutwell. She looked fairly well put together, considering. Actually, all the ladies in the room looked like they had freshened up. I had to hand it to them. The last thing I wanted to do after staring down the center of a tornado was slather on a fresh coat of face powder.

Mrs. Nutwell held up her hand. "So, I've been in touch with Ivan. He runs the scheduling and he says that we won't be able to have the auction at the event space anytime soon. As we all know, the golf carts really need that upgrade, so we need to troubleshoot and brainstorm some ideas here."

And then the talking got mumbled from my side. So many people had something to say at once, it became a mud of unintelligible words. I sighed. The obvious answer was to have the auction but not the party.

"Maybe just do it online."

Something must have quieted down the other side of the call, because my words were repeated by Mrs. Nutwell, followed by, "Who said that?"

When no one piped up, I said it again. "Just hold the auction online. Then you can still use all the organization you have in place for the event. At least it doesn't go to waste, right?"

The discussion on the other side started again, and my internet cut in and out. Eventually, I hung up my side, as it wasn't making any sense. I texted my sister a thumbs-up by way of thanks for the use of her device.

Upgrading the golf carts just didn't seem important enough to go balls to the wall on this auction. I'd honor my commitment if it came to that, but this all seemed liked it was doomed to fail.

BEAR

I tapped my fingers on my closed laptop while Burnie and I sipped a beer.

"So that's my offer."

It'd been a bold one. Burnie wanted to absorb Hanning Electric and expand his business. I tipped my beer back and focused on the hops on my tongue.

It felt scary to consider it. The lump sum Burnie was offering would be a great boost for my parents. I still had the fear in the pit of my stomach that my father may someday need more surgery or extreme health care.

"Think about it. If you want to take on Hanning for good, then great. We can work together when it fits. But I'd also take on your client list." Burnie shrugged.

Was selling out the business that provided for an ideal childhood and happy home life for me the right move? I mean, I'd have to talk to Mom and Dad. What I did like was that Burnie was a good guy and a great electrician. Our customers would be safe, as long as he had enough manpower to monitor them and serve any emergencies.

"You can stay on as long as you'd like, Bear. You're amazing and up on all the newest tech. You'd be an asset for sure." Burnie held up his glass for a toast. "Sorry this has to come on the heels of such a horrible storm."

It was something to consider. Though my other option would be my art full time. And that was possibly scarier than the tornado.

CHAPTER 31

MONDAY

*W*hen Bear made it back from his meeting with Burnie, he was very thoughtful and quiet.

I was more than happy to use everything but my voice to cheer him up. After two orgasms and a few new positions, he and I were curled up on the hotel couch together, naked.

"I told them to do it online and then the connection cut out, so I hung up." I traced his bicep with my finger.

"That's a great idea. I hope they listen to you." He watched my finger as it began to outline his chain tattoo.

"What about you?" I didn't want to pry, but something was eating him; I could tell from the faraway look in his eyes.

"Burnie wants to buy out Hanning Electric." He tilted his head one way and then the other as if the decision was shifting weight in his head.

"And that's got you flummoxed because…" I wanted to lead him into the conversation and the feelings without putting words in his mouth.

"One of the gifts that my dad is most proud of is giving me the business. The ability to be my own boss. And it's been in our family for three generations." His glance drifted to the electrical outlet in the room.

"You know, it's okay if the knowledge you gained there helps you evolve into another career. Your parents are going to love you and be proud regardless. You have to know that." I put my head on his shoulder and watched as he swallowed.

"Yeah. I guess the hard part with my parents is they would never discourage me from doing anything, even if it was secretly breaking their hearts. They'll always put my needs before theirs. So, they're actually not good people to go to for advice, because they won't weigh in advocating for themselves."

That sounded lovely. I didn't mention that his dynamic with his family sounded so healthy and ideal. Sure, we grew up in the pricey part of town, but Bear would never see his parents betray him. "Maybe put some time in, think about it. Did Burnie give you a deadline?"

Bear rested his hand on my hip. "No. He didn't. He seemed to want to give me time to think. And that's what I'll do. Before I talk to my parents, I'll really put in the time and try to figure out what makes the best, long-term financial decision. I want to make sure it's helpful to them."

"You rock. What a great son. And a friend to them. It's truly lovely." I leaned forward and kissed his jaw. The current state of our nakedness got us started again. I could not get enough of this man.

MONDAY

I knew avoiding my mom and dad for a week was probably

not the most mature maneuver, but once I was back in my apartment and feeding Mr. Nuts, I was having trouble getting up the guts to call them and ruin my night with what would be a fight.

But eventually, Mrs. Nutwell's email made plans for me. They must have decided to run with the online idea, because the email was brimming with graphics and login information. I made sure to follow the links and sign up in the required places.

Bear was flat out staying at my place now, but he'd cover up before going in and out. His hoodie was always pulled up. It was fine with me. It was a struggle not to paint him now that I had him and there was still space on my walls.

He was thinking. Making a big decision. I tried to help where I could.

The evening before the online auction, he was sitting on the couch, holding the remote, but the TV was off. I was grading papers at the dining room table.

I glanced at my phone and checked the time. Once it had been ten minutes, I set the papers aside. When I sat down next to him, I took the remote out of his hand and put it on the coffee table.

He sighed and rolled his head in my direction. "Was I creeping you out?"

I rubbed a hand on his thigh. "A little. I felt like I dragged a mannequin home from Old Navy. And I don't trust those guys at all."

He gave me a hint of a smile. "I think I know what I want to do, but I don't want to do it." He covered my hand with his.

"Did you stumble on the answer that I've known this whole time?" I tucked my legs underneath me and pushed myself closer so our foreheads could touch.

"Probably. I just feel like it is against my DNA to disappoint them. Dad has been looking forward to this his whole life. And I almost just lost him. I mean, the heart attack..." He rubbed the heel of his hand up and down the five o'clock shadow on his jaw.

"Hey. I haven't known them my whole life like you, but I think it's against *their* DNA to be disappointed in you. Honestly, they seem like the type of people who would hate that you were putting yourself through this." I put my hand on his cheek and rubbed the stubble with my thumb. "And isn't your dad doing great? Like really good?"

"He is. He totally is. It's like a miracle." He made eye contact with me.

"You need to let them know, then you can move forward." I put my hand on his chest.

"You're right. I know." He opened his arms completely and I curled into his chest. "It's hard to do the hard stuff."

"It always is. But you don't have to do it alone. I'm here." I listened to his heartbeat.

"Thank you." He squeezed me harder.

BEAR

I was in love with Monday Blue. Not just because she said she would be here for me, but that I knew she meant it.

She was exactly what I needed. Hell, she was what the world needed. Her beautiful heart was a wonder. The way she talked about her students, how concerned she was about them every day—it was what made the world turn.

I had to take it as a sign that telling my parents I wanted a different situation was the right move. I knew I was in love seconds after coming to the decision. And I knew my parents would love the love.

I kissed the top of Monday's head, and then I tipped her chin up so I could kiss her lips.

"Thank you," I said again. This time it was for existing. For being so incredible in my life. I wanted the moment I declared my love for her to be all about her, though. So instead of using words, I made love to her instead. I watched her feel without restraint as she orgasmed under my hands. Then I made sure to have it happen all over again while I was inside of her.

I was so in love.

CHAPTER 32

MONDAY

*S*omething had changed for Bear. I saw his shoulders relax and he even whistled when he was in the kitchen making us popcorn. I was grateful because he was obviously tearing himself up about the decision to pursue his art. And that was something I understood. My mother had been against my teaching job, so I knew feeling out of step with your family was hard. It had to be even harder for Bear because his parents were sensible.

I sent Bear a few texts with hearts as I thought of him throughout the next day. I had a professional day, so I reorganized my classroom. I had time to review the auction event for tonight. I was going to be live with Mrs. Nutwell for my auction. She wanted me to dress for success, which was hilarious. Dressing for success while painting for me was an old sweatshirt and leggings.

I was sure her definition was different. She wanted me to upload a few samples of my art, and she explained my pieces from previous auction winners would be displayed in a slide show. I picked a few different examples: some flowers, a bridge, and an edgy piece that reminded me of a nightclub. I was all set for the evening when it was time to go to the library for a staff meeting. There were new protocols for signing kids out of a building, so I knew it would be a long meeting. I sent Bear a kissy face before I went in.

My principal, Ms. Turvley, was holding court in front of the Smartboard. I sat next to the music teacher, Minnie, and made a promise not to chat in my head. I really liked Minnie to BS with. She shot me a wink and I knew she had the same thought.

"Thank you, guys, for coming today. We have a list to accomplish and I will try to get through everything quickly."

The PowerPoint on the board scrolled through some safety requirements for the kids and double-checking parent pickups at the playground at the end of the day.

Low in the pit of my stomach I felt something ominous. I looked outside. The weather was perfect. No sudden storms or anything that would make me concerned about lightning.

I brushed it off. After Ms. Turvley closed out our meeting, we chitchatted as a group for a bit. Minnie and I discussed our plans for the weekend. She was both attending a concert and performing at one. I was unable to attend because of the auction, but I wished her the best as we headed out of the library.

It's a habit for teachers to turn off the lights and close the door when exiting a room, and I was the last to leave. I got a text from Bear just before I hit the light switch and paused.

Minnie reached back and hit the switch. The snap and jolt were so loud, I jumped out of the way. I watched as Minnie crumpled to the floor.

"Don't touch anything!" I wasn't sure what happened, but I recognized the sound, and combined with my eerie feeling, it had to be electrically based. "Call 911."

The good news about teachers was they usually stayed cool in unexpected situations. In no time, the school nurse was all business with Minnie. I stayed with Minnie and held her hand. She was breathing, just flattened out by the jolt.

I looked at the switch. It was supposed to be me. I was the one that it was supposed to take down. I made sure Minnie had her phone, and then I moved out of the way as the paramedics arrived.

We were carefully cleared out of the building by the fire department. I didn't like it. Not one bit.

BEAR

I was standing in front of my parents, my armpits and hands sweating, when Monday's kissy emoji came through. I took a deep breath to settle my nerves.

My mother patted my shoulder and encouraged me to sit. "Bear, what has you so worked up?"

"How do you know I'm worked up?" I took a seat at the kitchen table across from Dad.

"A mother knows, sweetheart. You're sweating like we locked you in a sauna. You don't sweat unless you're nervous." She sat down as well, coffee mug in hand.

Dad added, "That's how I knew you were calm around electricity. If you were sweating, I would have never pushed you. Remember how scared you were of horseback riding when you were a kid?"

"Those animals are too big, and they don't even know it." I felt my pulse pound at the thought of the giant beasts.

"Well, when I placed you in front of your first fuse box, you were dry as a bone." He tapped his fingers on his temple and gave me a big smile.

It was the perfect opening and I had to take it. "About Hanning Electric—since we're on the topic." I watched as my dad's bushy eyebrows lifted, encouraging me to continue. It all came out as one big word. "IwannadomyartfulltimeandmaybenotrunHanningElectric."

I pushed my lips closed and waited to see what they would say. Maybe I should have eased into it. Hell, it might be a shock for my dad, and the last thing he needed was a shock right now.

Dad reached his hand across the table to my mom, and she took it. They were both smiling. I looked from one face to another. Something was up.

"We figured as much, Bear." Dad turned his attention to me. "Burnie contacted me and asked about purchasing the business. And I think it might be the right move."

My eyes were wide. "You already made the decision?"

Dad shook his head. "Of course not. We wanted to discuss it with you. Burnie gave us a very generous offer, but I'd never make a decision like this without you. And I wanted to make sure you were ready for that. You've known your whole life that the company was yours, so I didn't want to pull that away from you."

"It's not. I mean… not like you're pulling it away from me. Is my career as a furniture maker even sustainable? It makes me happy, but so does watching football on Sunday." I wiped my hands on my jeans.

Mom rolled her eyes. "You making furniture is on a totally different level. And if you want to see if it's a career, you're going to have to put a career's worth of effort and time into it."

She had a point. A great point. Dad was still smiling. "I just never want to disappoint you guys. And the business has been in the family…"

Dad lifted his hand to stop me. "Don't forget, you have all the knowledge you need and the last name if you want to start Hanning Electric up again down the line. Burnie will be buying my client list but using his own company name still. It's a perfect way for you to give your art all you've got. We'll keep the business running in name and paperwork, but only if it makes sense for you."

I looked at the table. They'd made this easy for me, of course. I didn't know why I expected anything else. They'd always put me first. Even now, as a grown-ass man.

I pushed myself away from the table and came around so I could embrace them both. "I love you guys so much, and I just want to make you proud."

Mom patted my shoulder and leaned her head against my cheek. "You've done that for us your whole life, and there's no stopping that ever."

Dad slapped my back. "What your mom said. We love you, son."

"Guess what?" Now that I had released my worry like a balloon, I wanted to share. "I'm in love with Monday."

My mom gasped and turned to give me a full hug. "I knew it! What did I tell you, honey?"

Dad chuckled, "Yeah. When you know, you know."

MONDAY

I put the finishing touches on my hair but planned to use a filter for my makeup. There were perks to having an online event. And that meant no heels as well. I texted Minnie, who was home and well. She was cracking jokes, so I took that as a good sign. I made a mental note to tell Bear about the situation as soon as the event was over.

I came out to the living room where Bear was having his Friday night beer. My black dress was unzipped. "Can you get this for me?"

I turned in front of him as he scootched up on the couch to help me. I felt his lips on the small of my back instead of the zipper closing.

"We do not have time for that. And you need to stop because you know you can convince me." I looked over my shoulder at him. He hung his head for a minute before trailing his knuckles down my spine, then carefully moved up the zipper. Then he grabbed my butt.

"You look amazing." He sat back and spread his arms on the back of the couch. I looked at the clock. I had a few minutes before I had to check in.

I sat in his lap and he wiggled his eyebrows at me. "You're so chill now. I'm thrilled your conversation went well with your parents."

"It did. You were right and they're the best, for sure. I'm really excited. Burnie said he'll use me as a contractor whenever I need extra money, so this is as risk-free as it could possibly get to start working on my furniture full time." Bear kissed my cheek. "I love when you don't have makeup on. I get to kiss anything I want."

"As soon as this is over, I want to take you up on that threat." I kissed his mouth for a little longer than I should.

As I pushed away, he smacked my butt again. I gave him a seductive look as I took up my spot in the corner of the living room. I set up my laptop and made sure my ring light was focused. I picked a light makeup filter and ran through my notes. I just had to introduce myself and give a short background of my work as an artist. Mostly, people who attended the event already knew who I was.

I had to hand it to Mrs. Nutwell. She knew how to hire people. The tech crew was soothing and had an official countdown.

When it was my turn to talk, I gave my intro, and before I was settled into the small talk, the auction started.

I muted my mic while the auctioneer did her work. The bidding started slowly. Then as time went on, the increments went up in bigger chunks. Last year, my session went for $35,000. We cruised right past that milestone.

As the number escalated, Bear stood just off-camera to watch. It was a cool 50k before the bids slowed down. A bidder I didn't recognize, Farn Mehorn, was the winner.

I waved and smiled at the number and then went off-camera. I received an email from the company that was running the auction for the Nutwells:

Dear Ms. Monday Level,

Thank you so much for participating in the auction for Hartford Greens. We are pleased to say that your auction session has been purchased by Farn Mehorn. We will be in contact with the details at a later date.

Sincerely,

High Value Auctions

"WELL, CONGRATULATIONS, BEAUTIFUL." Bear stepped around to pull me into a hug.

"Yeah, that's a lot of money. I really wish it was for something more...important." I jumped a little and Bear grabbed me by the butt so he could plant a kiss on my lips.

"I understand that. And maybe someday we can have you do it for a more special reason."

Bear walked me to the couch, and then I was straddling his lap while he sat. "Right now? Your business on the top, lounge on the bottom style is turning me on."

I laughed as he nibbled his way up my neck. "My intended purpose all along."

CHAPTER 33

MONDAY

Our weekend was a plethora of eating in and getting eaten out. Both were fabulous. On Sunday night, Bear was in gray sweatpants and nothing else but a big grin.

I was sitting crisscross on the kitchen counter wearing a matching pair of sweatpants and nothing else as well.

He came close and put his hands on either side of me on the counter. "I've been thinking."

He paused to trail kisses down my jaw.

"You're doing better than I am, that's for sure." I leaned into him.

"When's your lease up on this place?" He pulled away and looked around.

"I'm month by month. My dad's lawyer arranged it so my mom could hold out hope that I'd quit teaching and come back home to be a modern-day debutante." I glanced around with him. The walls alone were like living inside an artist's portfolio.

"Would you consider moving in with me? My walls are a

blank canvas, and I'd love to not hide the fact that we're together every time I duck in and out of the place we're staying." He closed one eye like he was taking a risk, but my heart knew otherwise. He could always bet on me.

"Sure." I leaned forward and kissed his nose. "Sounds great."

He lifted his eyebrows. "Really? Hot damn. Wow. That was easy!"

I uncrossed my legs and wound them around him. "I'll always be easy for you, babe."

And just like that, the deal was sealed. I'd move out next month and move into Bear's unconventional studio. The only problem I would have would be leaving Mr. Nuts. Oh, and my mother losing her ever-loving mind.

I never did get around to telling Bear about Minnie.

CHAPTER 34

$\mathcal{T}$he day of the auction session, I drove to the Nutwells' guest house. They were providing the space for the portrait painting. I would've really rather not traveled to see the Nutwell family again, but Nancy Nutwell eased my mind, saying the family was on holiday in Paris. Their home was about halfway between Mom and Dad's house and my apartment. Well, my empty, bland apartment. Bear and I had to paint over all of my art. We documented each piece extensively and polished off two bottles of wine as we covered over all my hours and hours of hard work.

He'd worked with his father on making some space for my stuff. Mr. Hanning was doing fabulous. They were still in the process of the sale to Burnie, but retirement suited the older Hanning very well. He was keen on Bear's tables, spending time running over the tops with his hand.

I was looking forward to spending time in my new space, close to Bear. And sure, I had a sneaking feeling that electricity had delivered me Bear as a bait and switch. And maybe it was planning on turning me into a barbeque when he was looking in the wrong direction, but also, I was facing my fear of the zappy stuff by planning on living amongst it.

Mrs. Hanning had taken to the idea of transferring Mr. Nuts to the meadow behind Bear's place. She was currently building a little house for the squirrel and had been doing a ton of research on squirrel relocation.

All in all, things were going great. I stopped myself from dwelling on my parents, and more specifically, my mother. I was going to get to that eventually.

As I pulled up to the Nutwell guest house, I dug my phone out of my art bag. The passcode for the gate was six numbers long and I had to enter it twice.

They were big on security, it seemed.

When I parked outside the "guest house," I realized that the Nutwells had more money than I had thought about. This so-called little place outside the city with the good light was a straight-up estate.

Mother would've loved it. Then she would have seethed that this was the Nutwells' spare house.

I parked my car in the roundabout and popped the trunk. I had the canvas delivered last week, so all I needed were my supplies.

Soon, I heard the front door open. I turned to see a well-dressed man. "Ms. Level? We've been expecting you. Please allow me to assist you with your belongings."

He was tall with a full head of gray hair. I stepped to the side with only my messenger bag slung over my shoulder.

"I'm Barker. If you need anything during your stay here, please don't hesitate." He lifted my bags that were full of paints and towels—pretty much everything I needed to do the whole damn job here today.

"Thank you. I'm looking forward to meeting Mr. Mehorn."

I watched as a bit of confusion clouded Barker's face. He recouped quickly. "Let me take you to the parlor."

I followed Barker up the stairs and through the large front door. The foyer looked like it could be in a public library. It was towering and stocked with tons of books. There was a clear aesthetic the house was modeled after. Like a cottage core theme if you had forty million dollars to waste.

The parlor was a dream come true, lighting wise. The floor-to-ceiling windows allowed the purest sun to highlight the room. I gasped quietly, thinking about capturing it.

"Lovely, yes?" Barker gave me a small smile.

"Very perfect. This'll be great. I need maybe twenty minutes to set up, but Mr. Mehorn can come in anytime. It's just him, correct?" I plopped my bag down and unzipped it.

"Yes. Mr. Mehorn. Very well." Barker slightly bowed to me and slipped out the open doors of the parlor.

It was weird how he was acting. But maybe that's how butlers behaved here in the Nutwell place. I had enough to keep me occupied as I set up my brushes and paints so that I didn't worry about it. Then I used the furniture in the room to create the look I wanted for Mr. Mehorn. I was looking forward to chatting with him a bit so I could infuse his personality into the work.

The large pendulum clock hit the top of the hour, and I was treated to the deep tones letting me know it was eleven a.m.

I started prepping my canvas. I could start working on the edges a bit while I waited.

I got lost in creating the sunlight, and I knew I was in my own headspace when a man cleared his throat. I jumped and jabbed myself in the cheek with a brush loaded with yellow paint. "Oh. Hi."

I reached down and grabbed my cloth, wiping the paint off. My gaze went from bare feet to bare legs.

Oh no.

At no point was it discussed that this would be a nude painting, but yup, that was a sack of nuts and a penis right there where they should be.

Instantly, I closed my eyes so all I could see were two slits framed by my lashes.

"Mr. Mehorn?" I held up a hand to block out his cock. When I got to his face, I dropped my hand. It was not anyone named Farn Mehorn.

It was Poncy Nutwell in his birthday suit. And a lit pipe.

"Are you serious?" I folded my arms over my chest and shook my head.

Poncy had enough sense to look ashamed, but he didn't cover himself either.

"Monday, good to see you. And yes, I'm serious. I purchased this experience, and I'm very much looking forward to it." He put one hand on his hip and tried to force himself to look comfortable.

"Does your mother know you're here, wearing nothing?" I waved my hand in his general direction.

"Well, she knows that I made this purchase, if that's what you're asking." He shifted his weight. I did my best to keep my eyes on his face.

"You know damn well that's not what I'm asking." I began to pack up my things. This guy. This guy right here.

"Wait, wait!" Poncy stepped closer.

I held up my paintbrush like a weapon. "Don't! Don't you dare. It's bad enough I have to look at it. You keep it where it is."

"According to the contract, I get to choose the attire for the session. You signed it. I signed it. This is all legally binding." He touched his head, and I noticed he was wearing a black beret.

"You're going to say that you chose the freaking hat?" I stopped packing up.

The last thing I wanted to do was be in a legal battle with the

Nutwells. Lord knows they had the money and the time to bury me.

"Yes. This portrait is very important to me." He scratched his stomach.

"Fine. Pose over there." I indicated the chaise lounge I had set up near the window.

Poncy puffed out his chest and looked proud of himself. I was so angry with him I felt like steam was coming out of my nose.

"How should I put myself? I want this to be very flattering, if you know what I mean. Fifty thousand dollars' worth of flattering." He wiggled his hips, and his dingle did a dongle.

"I paint realism. You'll get what you've got." I slid my lips to the side and wrinkled my nose. I had to paint him, but I wasn't required to be nice to him.

That statement caused Poncy to frown. "Fine. But do a good job."

I rubbed my hand over my mouth before approaching him. I could do this. I was a professional.

I told him to sit back and recline. Without having to touch him, I gave him instructions on how to place his feet and arms.

The awkwardness in the room was palpable.

I set myself up and tried to turn off the screaming in my brain. When Poncy took a bathroom break, I picked up my phone and texted Bear.

Farn Mehorn is really Poncy and he is having me paint him naked.

My phone rang almost immediately after the text message was shown as delivered.

"What?" Bear sounded completely shocked. There was also a lot of background noise. "How is that possible?"

I watched the door and spoke in a low voice. "He has a contract, and they have the money to fight me, so I think it's simpler to just do the painting and get out of here."

"Can you send me the contract?" Bear asked.

"Sure thing. And it looks like I have to get back to work." I ended the call and sent Bear's email the forwarded copy of the contract.

Poncy sat back down but required direction to be posed again. "I did a few push-ups out there, so please make sure to add that definition."

I let my face go blank.

"Or whatever. Listen, while you paint, I thought we could have a conversation." He tilted his hips and his penis flopped back into view as his centerpiece.

"It's better for the portrait if you stay as still as possible." I went to the window and pulled on the large drapery. The sun was moving and I wanted to keep the lighting as consistent as possible.

"I can do it without moving my mouth a lot." He tried to prove it to me to no avail.

"If you want this to be as flattering as possible, please stay still." I went back to mixing up the color for his knees. I was avoiding the bits and beans as long as possible. For now, I just had a few sketch lines.

The background was going to be amazing, and I could complete that at another time. I needed to bite the bullet and get to the problem area, though, so I started mixing the color for his man business.

Barker stepped into the room. "Mr. Nutwell, Ms. Level's assistant is here with the backup supplies she needed."

I watched as Poncy's face clouded with confusion. He had nothing on me because I'd never worked with an assistant before.

Bear walked in holding a bag and a lunchbox.

I looked from Poncy to Bear and back again. Poncy slid his legs to the side and used a pillow to cover up. "What's this all about?"

"I'm sure you've read the contract you signed, and it does allow for Ms. Monday Level to have an assistant accompany her." He moved close to me and set down the bags.

I watched as Poncy thought about his options. He had boxed me into doing this naked portrait, but thanks to Bear reading the contract, I was boxing him into having my boyfriend present during the painting.

I breathed a sigh of relief. It was lovely to not have to do this alone. The conversation Poncy felt he was entitled to was forced on the back burner.

"Of course, Ms. Level will need some lunch. Did you need to go get yours?"

Bear unraveled a paper-wrapped treat and I had to work at forcing my smile away. Bear had brought both him and me foot-long hotdogs for lunch.

Poncy seemed put out completely, which was understandable. He'd clearly set up the whole situation to make me as uncomfortable as possible.

I could just kiss Bear. And I did. When I looked back up, my subject had disappeared.

"How are you real?" I touched Bear's face.

"You're not alone." He turned his face to kiss my palm. He came away with a bit of pink paint.

Poncy came back with a silk robe on. "Can you work with what you've already done? Can I be done posing now?"

Poncy's neck and face had turned bright red.

I glanced at the picture. "For sure. I can finish this up and have it back to you next week."

If he hadn't trapped me here under false pretenses, I might've even felt a little bad for him. But...I'd had to see his peen. And now it was *in* a picture.

"Don't worry, Nutwell. If she needs a model, I can have her use my goods as a stunt double." Bear smiled widely at me.

I looked down for a few beats to keep my chuckle at bay.

Bear helped me clean up my area, and Poncy slunk out of the room while I was packing up.

I had to be careful with the wet canvas, but Bear's truck was the perfect place to stow it safely as we returned to his warehouse…well, our warehouse.

I followed Bear's truck in my car, and our cell phones were connected by speaker phone.

"You really showed up there today. I can't believe you."

"Are you mad? I'm sorry if that was out of bounds." He sounded slightly concerned as he pulled up to a red light.

I stopped my car a few feet behind his truck. "No, it was perfect. Honestly, I mean, I got to fulfill my end of the contract, and instead of Poncy making me uncomfortable, you switched it. I just love you so much." And then I stopped. I hadn't said that before.

I was waiting for his response, but he threw the truck into park and hopped out of it. I rolled my window down, concerned that there was a problem up ahead.

Instead, he grasped my face and laid the most passionate kiss on my lips. The honking snapped us out of our make-out session.

"The light's green," I offered, still lost in his eyes.

"They all suck and you're amazing. And I'm not going to even mention that you spent most of your day staring at another man's knob and grapes." He kissed me again, and another horn sounded.

Finally, the social pressure got to him. "I'll finish this when we get home."

A ride never took longer in my life.

CHAPTER 35

BEAR

*W*hen we were parked, I was out of the truck in a hot second, while Monday was just stepping out of her vehicle.

I had her pinned against it, my hands running up her sides as quickly as I could. My smile was threatening to overtake my face.

She wrinkled her nose at me and said it again without prompting, "I love you."

"Hey. I love you, too." I kissed her lips. Everything about Monday Blue matched what I was inside. I loved that she kept her word, even if it meant dealing with Poncy. I love that her job was literally helping bring color into the world for those who needed it most. I loved that she painted the door to the warehouse with a fall scene and two birds. One for her, one for me.

She dropped her purse to her feet and wrapped herself around me. She took a second to kiss each of my dimples and then my nose. She smoothed out my cheeks.

"This face is so important to my face."

"I totally get it." And the kissing against the car started again. It was actually getting too heated for as much clothes as we had on. "Care to take this inside?"

She nodded, her eyes bright. I reached down and grabbed her purse, making sure she had it secure, then I scooped her up in my arms.

"You're ridiculous." Monday started laughing, then settled into my arms and kisses.

I kicked her car door closed and made our way to the front door. I had to set her down to unlock the door, but I took the time to flip her ponytail out of the way and trail my lips up the back of her neck.

She walked through the door, even though I would've carried her. I was glad I didn't because I got to follow the trail of her clothes as she walked to the elevator. Her jacket, her shoes, her shirt, her bra.

When she got to the elevator, I was looking at a gloriously topless Monday with lust in her eyes.

"Sweet Christmas. When I die, I want this view to be my eternity." I made my way to her as quickly as I could. After getting two handfuls of her breasts, and kissing each nipple, I fell to my knees.

"Oh!"

She was surprised, but this woman loved me. And I knew she loved me too long without an orgasm, as far as I was concerned.

I dragged her leggings down with my thumbs, and her thong came with them, which saved me time.

Once I could touch her, I concentrated on tasting her. Long, slow laps with my tongue, followed by my fingers. The noises she made would have worried neighbors. Thankfully, we didn't have any because I wasn't stopping until she collapsed against me.

I felt her convulse around my fingers. I added some sucking to the services I was offering. I reached my free hand up and pinched one of her nipples. She writhed on my hand and her legs started to shake.

I took a breath to say, "That's it. Let it go." I licked my lips, then I went back in. I lifted her leg and put it over my shoulder. I could go deeper, and I did. My tongue was all the way inside of her as she gave a guttural moan mingled with my name.

When she went slack and boneless, I knew she was done. For the first time anyway.

She needed help getting her leg under her, and I made sure she didn't hurt herself as we both went to the floor.

We'd be making love. Because she loved me.

The fact that I thought I was in love before her was laughable now. Because now, I had Monday. The way she held everything for me was a rush. She had my hopes and dreams all along, I just needed to find her.

"I love you." I was going to say it too much, I already knew it.

"I can tell." She laughed, her voice thick with her exertions. "And I love you."

If people could hear us, they'd probably be rolling their eyes.

And then, she was pushing me flat on the floor. "Time for you."

I helped her slide my pants off my hips, and I was more than ready for her hands and mouth.

She was as creative down there as she was in the regular world, and I was grateful.

Between the nipping and incredible deep-throating, I was closer to the edge than I expected. Almost embarrassingly so.

"Wait. Stop." I pushed myself up on my elbows so I could see her.

She locked eyes with me but kept my dick in her mouth. I could feel her tongue swirling on the tip and my eyes almost crossed.

"It's going to happen. I'm going to come."

Monday raised one eyebrow and shrugged, and then she went faster and slightly deeper. I was done. As I came, she swallowed what I had to offer, all the while massaging my balls. Every muscle in my body was ready to snap. My screaming made her moaning even louder. She started to hum with me in her mouth.

I left my body. She reached up and pinched my nipple, and I knew she was making sure she was being fair.

When I stopped convulsing, Monday wiped her mouth and snuggled on my chest. I wrapped my arms around her.

"Are you kidding me?"

"Just giving what I'm getting. I think that's fair."

"More than fair." I kissed the top of her head. I was as happy as I could be. I squeezed her in a hug.

The rest of the night was a test of endurance and staying hydrated. We couldn't keep our hands off each other.

CHAPTER 36

MONDAY

*M*onday morning, I had to make sure to refill Mr. Nuts' little house. He was doing great here at the warehouse. There were more trees and space for him. I smiled to myself thinking about how I had taken to calling Bear Mr. Peen.

The weekend was everything. Being young and in love was a heady thing. And man, I had never been in love before. Not like this. There had been crushes, and of course, I thought some of my earlier boyfriends were the real deal, but Bear was a man. I respected his love of his parents and the way he saw to it that they were okay. The fact that he was leaning into his dream of making unique furniture. He was forever. I just knew it.

Just as I was thinking about him, I heard his boots on the gravel. "How's our favorite rodent?"

Bear slid his arms around my middle.

"He's great. Seems really happy here. Certainly eats a ton, though I think his friends are onto us as well."

I pointed out Mr. Nuts and he was frolicking with two other squirrels.

"That's awesome. I want to do a squirrel-inspired piece in his honor."

I turned in Bear's arms. "Can you add the fried chipmunk, too?"

"From the night we first met? Sure." Bear rocked back on his heels. "You know, it occurred to me that that little guy gave his life for our love."

"Aw, that's sad and lovely at the same time." I patted Bear's shoulders. "I've got to get going."

He kissed me for a few more minutes before walking me to my car. I loved my job, but Mondays were hard now that I wanted to spend every waking moment near Bear.

CHAPTER 37

BEAR

I was in deep with my sanding. My music was loud, and I was in the zone. Fine, I was thinking about Monday. I had been looking at a few pictures of her on my phone, so it was close when it rang. Monday was calling me, which was weird. I glanced at the time. Usually she was in class about now. And teaching a classroom full of kids was not the time to ring your guy.

I answered, "What's up?"

I didn't recognize the voice on the other end. "Hi, this is Minnie. You don't know me, but I know that Monday would want me to call you."

"What happened?" I had flashbacks to the call from my mom about my dad when he had his heart attack. There was just something that set my heart on edge.

"She's getting put into an ambulance. They're starting compressions. Her mother is headed to the hospital, but I wanted you to know."

I couldn't swallow. I couldn't speak for a second. Then I forced myself to be level-headed. "What hospital are they headed to?"

I didn't know what was wrong, but compressions were bad. That meant her heart. Her heart that I recently got to call my own was being forced to beat.

"Midiville General."

I hung up. I needed to get there immediately. I ran to my truck. It was freezing outside and I was just in my t-shirt. I had my phone navigate me to the hospital. I was pretty sure I knew how to get there but having the backup directions wasn't a bad thing because my head was everywhere.

I used voice dialing to call my mom. I needed to tell someone.

"Hey, sweetheart." She sounded so chipper.

"Mom." I could barely think of how to tell her what had happened. I knew nothing. Actually, worse than nothing. I only knew Monday was in dire trouble.

"What happened?" She could tell from my voice that I was beside myself.

"Monday's on the way to the hospital." The navigation directions interrupted me, and I followed them. As soon as Mom was done speaking, I resumed what I knew, "They were putting her in the ambulance and doing compressions."

"Oh my God." I heard Mom's sharp intake of breath, then she relayed what I said to my father. The navigation pinged in again. I ran a red light to follow what the GPS directed.

"Are you headed there now?" I could hear my mom's car keys jangling.

"Yeah. Midiville General." My voice cracked. *How was this reality?*

"We'll meet you there. Drive safely. That's the only thing you can do for Monday. Or do you want me to stay on the phone?" I heard a car door slam.

"No, I have to concentrate. Love you."

"I love you, too, Bear."

I was parking in the hospital lot, taking up two spaces, when I finally shut off the navigation. Déjà vu was slapping me in the face. I ran to the ER and to the receptionist. "Looking for Monday Blue Level?"

She started typing. I felt a hand on my shoulder. When I turned around, I saw Chestnut Level.

"He's with me." She looped her arm through my elbow. "He's family."

The receptionist nodded before handing me a sticker to write my name on, marking me as a visitor.

"How is she?" I snapped my eyes to Mrs. Level's face.

"She's okay. From what I gather, she was shocked at school by some faulty wiring, and her heart stopped. They had to use the defibrillator on her to get her rhythm back. But she is back. And she is resting."

I felt like my heart fell out of my chest. "She was dead?"

"Briefly. She's still with us." Monday's mother's eyes were rimmed in red. This was a different demeanor than I'd dealt with in the past from her.

"Can I see her?" I was now at her mercy. I wasn't sure where Monday was.

"Yes, this way." Chestnut led me to a curtained area. When I moved behind the curtain, seeing Monday's face was a balm on my ragged heart. She had a heart monitor on that was following a reassuring beat.

Her eyes fluttered open, and she held out her hand.

I grabbed it and leaned down to kiss it. "Babe, what happened?"

It felt like I'd been kicked in the feelings. No idea how a perfectly healthy Monday was now laid up in the ER.

She seemed tired but with it. "I was shocked. That's what they tell me anyway. I was plugging in my computer charger, and just, white and ouch, and the next thing I knew, I was coming to in here."

Chestnut rounded the other side of the bed and straightened the blanket by Monday's feet.

I pushed her hair out of her eyes. "How the hell? What the hell?"

Chestnut took over the details. "Well, I guess there has been some faulty wiring at the school, and just last Friday a teacher was shocked from a light switch. The building is old, and some repairs have been left by the wayside."

Chestnut's mouth turned down at the corners.

"It hit you so hard your heart stopped?"

Monday closed her eyes and nodded. "Yeah. That's what they say. I told you all electricity hated me, but I think we're cool now. Like it got me out of its system. They used the defibrillator on me, so it took electricity to get me back." She took a deep breath and held my hand tightly. "Can you stay?"

"I wouldn't be anywhere else." I found the closest chair and hooked it with my foot, dragging it until I could plop down.

Chestnut adjusted the blanket again and went close to the IV bag that was hanging near the bed. "They're going to have to refill your saline bag next time they come around, I think."

Monday was already asleep, so I nodded at Chestnut so she'd know someone had heard her. "I can't believe this happened." I said it more to myself, but Chestnut responded.

"Me either. Thank God she's still with us. I think I saw my whole life collapse in front of me."

The doctor peeked into the curtained area. "How's she doing?" A nurse trailed behind.

While the doctor checked Monday's vitals, the nurse made notes and then swapped out the saline bag.

"Anything we need to know?" I leaned forward.

"Well, sir, I've spoken to Mom here, but I'd be happy to loop you in. Monday's system is recovering. Because of the severity of her shock, we're going to keep her with us, probably for a few days. She's young and very healthy, which is all in the plus column. With shocks of this nature, we like to be cautious and make sure there are not any secondary issues. She'll need to keep up a dialogue with the cardiologist. We'll examine her eyes and hearing—honestly, just the works. I've seen some tough shocks in my day, and hers was rough, but not the worst." The doctor turned her gaze to Monday who opened her eyes.

"Hey, Doc. How's it going?" Monday moved her hands over her bedsheet.

"Good. What's your pain level from one to ten—ten being the worst?" The doctor started typing on a small laptop.

"I'm good. I have a bit of burning sensation in my chest, and my legs feel sore. I'd put it all together as a three." Monday looked at me and I smiled at her.

"That's reasonable. We're going to keep asking you that question for the length of your stay." The doctor looked in Monday's eyes and ears. "I don't want to get ahead of myself, but I think you're going to recover just fine from this. We won't take any chances, but I think you all can start to breathe easy." The doctor spoke quietly to Chestnut, who murmured her thanks.

I felt like I could finally inhale. I called my parents and my mom picked up before the first ring was over. "She's okay."

"Oh, thank heavens. She's okay, sweetie." I heard Mom tell Dad the good news. "We're out here in the parking lot. You just take your time in there, but if you need us, we're here."

Monday squeezed my hand. "Go talk to them, the little sweethearts. Please tell them I'm sorry I scared everyone."

"You have nothing to be sorry for." I looked at Chestnut. "You staying here?"

Chestnut nodded. "I'm not going anywhere until someone makes me."

She fussed with Monday's blanket again. I recognized the

fight of a mother in Chestnut and was happy to see it, though sorry for the life-threatening situation that brought it about.

"Okay, I'll be back in a few minutes." I kissed Monday's forehead. I had every intention of crying in my mother's arms.

MONDAY

Mom was the most present she'd ever been in my life. She was one hundred percent laser-focused on me. It was weird. It was definitely motherly.

My mother's FaceTime started ringing. She answered it and I got a good view of my father's chin. He didn't seem to understand where the camera was on the phone, but I was too tired to try to fix it for them.

"Can you hear me?" he boomed into the microphone.

"Yes, dear, are you on the way home?" She sat in the chair that Bear had recently vacated.

"I'm about to get on the plane. Did you see her? Can I talk to her?" Dad was holding the phone upside down, but I could see his eyes now.

"Yes, here she is."

Mom attempted to reverse the camera but kept pressing it twice in a row, evening up looking at her own face every time. I held out my hand.

She passed her phone to me, and I gave my dad my best smile.

"Oh God, you look so tired. How are you feeling, baby girl?" Dad leaned close to the camera and I was treated to an up-close nostril shot.

"You haven't called me baby girl in about twenty years. Are you okay?" I wanted to tease him, but it was also true. He hadn't used my nickname in a long time.

"I'm not okay. They were telling me your heart stopped!" Dad got his face more in focus and his eyes were wild. "What the hell happened?"

I thought back to the incident. It seemed years away even though it was only hours. "I was at school, in the library for a quick staff meeting, and my laptop needed to be charged. I grabbed my charging cord, unraveled it, and plugged it into the wall before plugging the end into the computer. I'm not sure that's the reason, but then everything seized up and went white. When I finally understood where I was, I was here in the hospital."

"I'm going to sue anything that holds still. That is the most asinine setup in the world if you can get a shock so severe they literally have to bring you back to life." Dad's neck was red and I was getting concerned.

"Let's just have Monday get better before we worry about vengeance." My mother took the phone from me and gave my father a harsh look.

"Okay. Okay. I'll be there as soon as possible. I love you, Monday." My dad had wet eyes, which in turn had me tearing up.

Mom ended the call, and then she put her phone away. She messed with the blanket at my feet again.

"I'm good, Mom. I haven't even moved and you've fixed my blanket three times." I was too exhausted to fight her, but I had to point out how weird she was being.

Mom looked at the ceiling and then the floor. She was quiet for an extended period before she finally got to what was bothering her.

"I'm sorry. I'm so sorry I made it seem like the Nutwell last name was more important than you. I was wrong. I was so wrong." Mom sobbed and hugged herself.

"Oh, Mom." I held out one arm to her and she collapsed into my arms. I winced and she pulled her weight off of me.

"Sorry. I just… when they called me from the school, I'd never been so scared in my life. And the whole way here, I kept saying, 'I'm not giving up. Not giving up on Monday.' And foolishly, I thought, it's her day of the week. No one can die on their day of the week." Mom sniffled.

I pointed to the tissues on my end table. She reached over and swiped one.

"Hey. I'm here and I'm okay. We're going to be okay." I patted her shoulder.

"We will be okay. And I have to make some changes because I had a lot of regrets on that ride over here." Mom held my hand, and I was a little bit leery, but it seemed like she was being real. It sucked that I had to basically die for her to realize that her daughters are more important than status, but if that's a good thing that came out of this weirdness, then at least it was a positive.

CHAPTER 38

BEAR

I was staring at the large painting of a naked (sans penis) Poncy in my house. Somehow, his wang became my responsibility. Monday was concerned about meeting her deadline, even though Poncy had emailed her with an extension when he'd heard she was in the hospital.

Monday had begged me to finish the painting however I could and drop it off with the butler. So this was why I was trying to picture in my mind's eye what Poncy's man dongle looked like. When I had visited Monday while she was painting him, I glared at his gummy worm a few times to try to make him as uncomfortable as he had made Monday.

But honestly, I didn't commit it to memory. I held a paintbrush in my hand and pointed it at his likeness. "Prince Asshole von Testes, I hate you. And I can't paint. And I sure as shit can't paint your slim jim."

I growled at the painting. Monday had done a magnificent job capturing the essence of Poncy's swarmy entitlement.

I had an idea. A slow, stupid idea that would give me great pleasure, and with my girlfriend spending her last night in the hospital, I was due a little pleasure.

After discarding the paintbrush, I set to work with the tools of my trade.

It had taken all night. And at seven forty-five a.m., I was exhausted, but I was done. I took a video of the completed work and a few pictures so I could show Monday later today.

After wrapping the painting in bubble wrap, I packed it into my truck. I'd drop off the painting and be home in time for Monday's arrival. Her parents wanted to drive her home from the hospital, and I agreed to let them do it.

I texted Monday that I couldn't wait to see her and got on the road. My instructions were to deliver the painting to the butler Barker. When I got there, Poncy was in the doorway.

"How's Monday?"

I didn't feel like he was entitled to anything as far as Monday was concerned.

"She's fine. Here's your art. Now she's done with you." I slid the framed piece out of the truck. Barker appeared with a rolling dolly.

"I'd like to do the unveiling in private, Barker, in the same room we did the session." Poncy swished his hips as he led me to the parlor again. I set the painting against the wall and took out my pocketknife.

I sliced the bubble wrap off and revealed the art. I stood back, wondering if I'd been delusional. The only way I could complete the painting for Monday was using the only art I knew. I framed the painting in wood that I hit with electricity to make the Lichtenberg pattern, then I had it snake up the canvas and end in a spectacular fashion on Poncy's crotch. So instead of a penis, he looked like he had a bolt of lightning as a dick.

I heard his gasp. I reluctantly looked at his face, prepared to hear the complaints. He had one hand over his mouth. I stood waiting. And then he dropped his hand and put it between his legs, cupping himself.

"That's incredible. I can't... I just love it so much. I was expecting the worst, considering..." Poncy started moving to different parts of the room to get different views. Then he went into the hall and called in Barker. "Can you even stand it? How incredible!"

The butler gave the painting a satisfied nod. "Ms. Level is very, very talented."

I didn't detect a lie. The butler really loved it.

Poncy pointed at the painting. "That's the best fifty thousand I've ever spent."

He seemed to forget himself and came over, offering his hand for a limp shake.

"Glad it works for you. I'll leave you to it." I let go of Poncy's hand and motioned for the butler to lead me out.

Barker commented as we made our way back to the front door, "That's some serious skill. I wish Ms. Monday Level the best."

I nodded at him and went back to my truck—piece of penis art forgotten. I was getting my girl back and I couldn't wait.

MONDAY

My parents were overcompensating, but I didn't mind. Mom had a car service for us all to go to my place with Bear. She had argued that she should take care of me at home, which made me laugh. Because the place was so big, it'd be a lot just to go from the kitchen to my room a few times a day.

And as great as it was that my mom had arrived at a new approach to her parenting, I wanted to be at home with the man I loved. When we got to the warehouse, Bear was waiting with a huge smile.

He looked sexy and overjoyed. He met me at the passenger door and opened it. I had a clean bill of health, with caution to take it easy for a few days and check in with my general practitioner in a week.

I wasn't on pain meds. The cardiologist was happy with my tests, and the respiratory therapist told me that I was breathing like a champ.

It appeared that I was one of the lucky ones when it came to a serious shock. After I finally convinced my parents to leave, Bear took me on the elevator. I snuggled into his chest.

"I used waterless shampoo last night and I can't wait to shower. Like, it's legit all I can think about."

"You can stink, you cannot, I'm just thrilled you're here." Bear held the elevator door open for me.

I walked into the main space and saw a glaring absence. "I'd like to see the Poncy piece."

"I... uh ... finished it and dropped it off already." He looked like he was afraid it was the wrong thing to do.

"You painted his penis?" I gestured toward my crotch.

"Sort of? I kind of turned it into a bolt of lightning and he was thrilled." He pulled out his phone and showed me the picture.

"Are you serious? You worked this hard on Poncy?" I touched the screen to zoom in on it. It was so intricate and massively worked in Poncy's favor. It was a genuine piece of art. The mixed media was the edge. "Stupid Poncy getting the most badass nude I've ever seen."

Bear smiled wide. "I'm glad you approve. I just wanted to close that contract out for you so you wouldn't have to deal with him again."

"That was thoughtful. I appreciate that so much." He was too much. The thoughtfulness killed me. "I'm going to shower and then I want to spend the night in your arms."

I nipped off to the bathroom and washed my hair for what felt like hours. The after-the-hospital shower was one of my top two favorite showers I'd ever had.

When I had on my softest pajamas, I ran into Bear at the bedroom door. "Hey."

"How was that?" He anxiously searched my face.

"It was no lightning bolt peen, but it was incredible." I was finally able to lay the love on Bear like I had wanted to before. My fresh face and brushed teeth made me feel unstoppable.

He was careful with me even though I promised him I was more than fine.

"I've got spaghetti and meatballs for us for dinner, if you're in the mood." He walked me to the dining room table.

"Let me at it." I slid onto the bench seat and touched the shape in the table. It was the one that was based off of my silhouette. So stunning.

Bear and I had our meal, but he pushed his food around like he was distracted.

"Everything okay?" I realized that things probably happened during my hospitalization. That he was subjected to dealing with my parents, who were insane but pretty devoted to me now. I hoped they hadn't turned him away from me somehow.

He ran a hand down his face. "Only one way to find out."

He pushed away from the table and got down on one knee. "Monday Blue, I've been crazy about you since you tried to bury that charred chipmunk with a spatula. Shit. That's not what I wanted to say." He tried again, this time grabbing my hand. "Ever since you came back to life, I've wanted to make sure you spent it with me. Monday, will you make me the happiest guy and become my wife?"

He reached into his pocket and pulled out an antique looking diamond.

I nodded, struck silent with emotion.

"It's my grandmother's ring, but if you don't like it—"

I found my voice to interrupt him. "It's amazing. You're amazing. Yes to you. Yes to us. Yes to this ring."

I tossed my arms around him and pulled him close.

"Really?" His eyes were sparkling.

"Really. Of course. I love you." I kissed his mouth.

"I love you, too."

EPILOGUE

The twins were sharing a cradle. Volt's hair was standing on end and Watts had the same style.

"I think their hair has everything to do with your profession." My mother tried to look down her nose at Bear, but he was much taller, so it didn't work out. She just looked like she was pointing her chin at him.

"Chestnut, I think they'll take after you. Check out that volume." Bear scooped up Watts and touched his head.

My father had clearly come into his own as a grandfather. He was currently reading a very newborn Volt a story. I wasn't sure that Volt was paying attention, but it was keeping my dad happy. Bear's parents were glowing. I swore they were each hovering a few inches off the ground.

Volt Brad Hanning and Watts Harry Hanning were a few weeks early, but that was to be expected. I had a few unplanned visitors by way of the hospital staff that took care of me after my shock. They were heroes and made for great ways to get some extra professional opinions on the health of the babies.

It'd been a whirlwind year and a half. I recovered from the shock quickly enough and went back to work. Bear insisted on having me smuggle him and his father in so they could fix the electrical problem at the school. Normally, the red tape and policies would take a long time to get everything in place, and I was grateful. I had to be able to plug things in and be confident that I'd be alive when I was done. The worker's comp claim was a process that was chugging along.

The elder Harry worked with me on designing a button-driven paint program for my kids. Leo and kids just like him would be able to add their touch to murals that we painted at school. It was amazing.

The wedding was in the warehouse, and my mother complained a little bit. She only invited the people in her life who would not be judgmental of a small, intimate ceremony. Minnie was there, and both of us were closer now that we had our shocks in common. Bear had constructed a beautiful wall piece for our wedding, and it served as a backdrop for all the pictures.

Another twist of fate was the success of Poncy's peen painting. What started out as a way for him to make me uncomfortable turned into the biggest advertisement for mine and Bear's combined services.

Shock 'n Paint was born. The Nutwells hung the portrait in a prominent spot in their main house. It was quite the showpiece and a great conversation starter. Soon we had emails from acquaintances and business partners of the Nutwells asking for portraits of their own. We made a stipulation that every commission had to donate supplies to my school program as well.

And soon after our wedding, on a random Friday night, I forgot to take my birth control. It was an honest mistake, and Bear was excited with the start of our family. Twin boys were both born with a full head of shocking hair, and both were spitting images of their father.

My sisters were proud aunts and my mother and father seemed to soften even more.

After tucking the boys into their crib in the nursery in the warehouse, I turned to Bear. "You changed everything for the better, you know that?"

He smiled like he knew, and it had been his plan all along. We kissed in the shadows of the night.

THE END

Want to read about Volt and Watts and their run in with Mr. Nuts' descendants?

I've got you covered! Join my newsletter for instant access: https://www.debraanastasia.com/flickerbonusscene

BOOTY CAMP DATING SERVICE

Sometimes we're not done!

Still in the mood for some more sweet, spicy rom com?

Check out Booty Camp Dating Service's First Chapter:

Clown Fetish

Hazel's throat was raw from screaming Scott's name. He did that to her. With his hands, his mouth, and his long, thin penis. She was lying on a towel which was wet enough to have soaked through to the mattress below. His sexual talents made her feel more beautiful than she'd ever felt before. Her eyes stayed closed, but she heard him rustling around. Her fingertips felt like rubber. Hazel touched the pad of her index finger to the nail on her thumb. He'd fucked the feeling out of her hands. She could sleep like this, splayed out on the bed, naked and rosy. She was betting her nipples were a hot red and might even match the marks he'd left on her ass cheeks.

Maybe even the blush on her face would match, too, as she thought of how, in between screaming his name, God's name, and a lot of guttural sounds, she'd told him she loved him.

That was not a step she'd planned to take while her ankles were on his shoulders, but when her body had been strung tight like a fist and he'd released it with a combo that should be in every boyfriend handbook, Hazel's mouth made its own decisions.

Scott was taking longer than he should have to bring back a warm, wet towel from the bathroom, so she forced herself to peel open at least one eyelid to check on him. He was buttoning his jeans.

Hazel let herself enjoy the sight of him—the bare chest and jeans was a classic combo, and he made it look good. She finally made it to his face and offered him a satisfied smile— he sure as hell had earned it.

Scott was stone-faced.

"You okay?" She was so boneless she couldn't even move yet, so her concern was only on her tongue.

"I'm leaving." He pulled his T-shirt over his head.

"Oh? Are you hungry? I can make something. I know you've got nothing to cook upstairs." She let her hand flop onto her stomach.

Just as she was thinking about how lovely it was that they were so comfortable naked with each other, he changed the atmosphere in the entire room. "No, I'm leaving you. This is over. I'm done."

Now Hazel was able to prop up on an elbow. Though the words were confusing and her brain was trying to wrap around what he'd said, it was his flat tone that had her heart pounding all over again—but for different reasons.

"You're going back to your apartment?"

The room's scent was so hardwired into her brain— telling her she was happy—that she just couldn't make the connections she needed to.

"I'm breaking up with you right now."

Hazel finally sat all the way up. "What?"

Scott was fully clothed now but picking up his shoes because apparently he was in such a rush that he couldn't take the time to put them on. Scott was at her bedroom door before he looked back over his shoulder.

She was in mid-crouch now, trying to gather her clothes. He took one last look at her naked, bent form.

"That last orgasm was my parting gift. I've got another girl. She lives on the top floor of this apartment. Don't make this weird for me, okay?"

Scott closed the bedroom door, and she sat on the floor, holding her pants and one sock. It took him a few minutes to close the front door. Later, she would figure out that he'd stopped to take the six-pack of beer he'd stashed in her fridge while they fucked.

And that's what they'd done. Scott had changed it on her, from making love to fucking.

It had been the first time she'd ever told a guy that she loved them.

And as she hugged her two articles of clothing to her chest, she promised herself it would be the last.

It wasn't until he was drilling his new girlfriend on her ceiling that she realized she needed to move out of her apartment. Well, it wasn't really on her ceiling, but on his floor that also happened to be her ceiling. No amount of screaming, loud music, or broom handle banging would make him stop. Or her. The new girlfriend had a super annoying habit. The harder she came, the harder she laughed. The shrill sound of her explosive laughter as Scott made every sex dream she'd ever had come true induced nightmares for Hazel. Very specific nightmares involving clowns in fetish gear.

She had to move. She had to get out.

It wasn't so easy to get the hell out of a one-year lease, and in her panic, Hazel had a moment of extreme insanity. Well, maybe it was a sleep-deprived decision made in anger and sadness. And a severe desire to be out from under Scott's hyena-pounding. When her best friend, Claire called screaming about winning a chance to be a part of Booty Camp, Hazel allowed herself to be swept away in her friend's excitement.

Booty Camp
Dating Service

Hazel Lavender gave her best friend, Claire Paquet, a hard look after she got the receipt from the car service driver.

"If my tits pop out of this top one more time, you owe me your firstborn child."

Claire patted the tops of her boobs like they were friendly pets. "Stay puppies. Good job." Then she turned her attention back to Hazel's face with some advice. "Just don't do any whore bends and you'll be fine."

Claire could convince a fish in a bowl to buy a bottle of water. Her friend's powers of persuasion had brought them to the front doors of the old movie theater downtown. Hazel wished the wine bottle they'd polished off at Claire's apartment while getting dressed had provided bravado with more staying power.

But all it had done was given her the courage to jam her breasts into a top owned by the slightly less-endowed Claire and call it sufficient.

But what do you wear to meet the love of your life?

That was the question the wine had answered.

The answer was a swishy skirt, a titty top, and high heels.

No jacket required.

As the chill from the evening breeze swept over her chest, Hazel seriously doubted the alcohol's qualifications to make that decision. Although she *was* enjoying feeling carefree and not giving a moment's thought to Scott and his upstairs hyena.

There was a single sign on the glass doors leading to the venue.

Welcome to Booty Camp Dating Service!

Claire pointed at it. "Well, we're in the right spot. Are you ready to fall in hopeless, orgasmic love?"

"It's convoluted. Like the Emperor's new clothes. This is a horrible idea, and you hate me." Hazel concentrated on getting up the cement stairs without falling. The whole building seemed like it had come from another time when everything was smaller. Dinner plates, drinks, and— apparently—stairs. There was a generous wheelchair ramp to the left of the entrance, and Hazel couldn't have been happier to see it there. She always noted when vintage buildings successfully retrofitted their accessibility options.

She sucked at heels. She so rarely wore them to work, but her tormentor/boss/best friend was smooth in them. Claire even had a pair of high-heeled sneakers. Now, she didn't wear them, but the fact that they existed and Claire felt compelled to own them really highlighted the differences in their personalities. And jobs.

Hazel was a third-year special education teacher, and Claire was her assistant principal. Claire was the perfect remedy to a soggy heart that had been screwed over too hard by Scott.

They had met at the pool back home years ago. Claire was six years older and had been the college-aged pool manager when Hazel arrived there for her very first job. They'd hit it off despite the gap in their ages.

But now, hurrying into the lobby of the theater to avoid the crisp breeze, they were far from the hot summer days of years ago.

Everyone in the lobby glanced over in the city way of checking them out without appearing to check them out. Hazel smoothed down the back of Claire's bright red hair where the elements had mussed it up.

Claire was talking to someone right off. She was just outgoing. And when she was nervous, she was even more outgoing. Hazel pulled her phone out of her purse and held it like a lifeline.

The room was full of single people looking for a connection. It felt like an odd mixture of *being* the steak fed to a group of sharks and fighting to get the last clearance dress at a sample sale. The competition and the want in the room were thick.

Smiling, attractive people wearing black T-shirts with "Booty Camp" emblazoned on them worked the room, holding out clipboards and pens.

Hazel looked at Claire as the tall, dark, and handsome Booty Camp Dating Service employee handed her two clipboards. She thanked him distractedly and narrowed her eyes at Claire when she placed her hand on the man's forearm.

It was the hook-up gesture. Hazel had been in too many bars when Claire was PMS-horny not to notice it was her signature move.

If Claire was really into the guy, she would comment on the strength and squeeze.

"Do you lift? My heavens, these are some firm muscles right here."

Bingo.

Hazel was too intimidated to glance around again. She started filling out her permission, as it were. She added the usual: her name, number, and profession. There were no leading questions. She expected a ream of paper that grilled her on egg preference and her favorite bands, but instead, Booty Camp got right to the good part—writing out a check. She could have swiped her card on the payment square each Booty Camp employee had on their phones, but Hazel's father's distrust of all cellular devices and scams made her decide to go the paper route.

One thousand dollars. She gave Claire the evil eye that the woman missed. Hazel made out her check grandma style and clipped it to the board before passing it back to the smiley Booty Camp girl who introduced herself as Alison. The staff member had a fancy camera that printed out an instant candid snap of Hazel, and she clipped that to the board before it had even developed.

At this point, Claire was flat-out canoodling. Hazel had never seen anything that would fit the definition before in person, but Claire had her boobs propped up like two parrots on the guy's forearm while fluttering her eyelashes. Said guy was built—tall and looked a lot like Gaston from "Beauty and the Beast." He was the exact opposite of Claire's type. She was always looking for waif-like, pained blond dudes. This guy was masculine with a capital Balls. Hazel felt her jaw drop when Gaston waved away the Booty Camp girl as she tried to give Claire a clipboard.

"This one is comped." He smoldered at Claire like they were both wearing matching satin jock shorts.

Her assistant principal best friend, who handled just about any human with an efficient business tone, giggled like she was getting her armpits tickled. When Gaston sidled closer to swing his giant arm around Claire's shoulders, Hazel saw he had the company logo on the back of his shirt, as well.

Claire's happy gaze fell on Hazel's face. Her friend mimicked grabbing Gaston's ass but stopped just short of doing so to show Hazel how interested she was in the man.

Hazel raised her eyebrows in acknowledgment. Claire always excelled. She was a driven lady. And if the goal was to get a man, well, it shouldn't surprise Hazel that Claire had completed the goal before she was even officially registered— and with an employee, no less.

Hazel looked around the room. All the people were fairly typical of those she would meet out on a Friday night. They were stylish and corporate-looking.

On the perimeter of the lobby, she spotted a guy who made her feel something other than awkward embarrassment. Now he was mouthwateringly hot. Clearly he didn't belong—with his longish hair and high cheekbones. Even all the way across the room, she could tell his eyes were a piercing, hot blue. He was either wearing guy-liner and mascara or he had the kind of eyelashes that made every lady grit her teeth in jealousy. When he turned a little, she saw that he was wearing a shirt that matched Gaston's.

Hazel wanted to roll her eyes, but instead Claire caught her by her upper arms and shook her.

"I bet his man salami is like a fist!" Claire was flushed and her eyes were sparkling.

"If you tell me you're in love, I'm going to punch you in the vagina."

"I'm in love."

"Son of a bitch."

Claire started filling Hazel in on all the details she'd been able to glean from Gaston during their four-minute relationship, but Hazel tuned her out and peered over her shoulder.

Guy-liner was making his way over to Gaston. She wanted to hear his voice. Not that she was checking him out— because she certainly wasn't.

His dark jeans and motorcycle boots were not similar to the other employees' attire. He was having some strong words with Gaston. Hazel tuned in and overheard:

"No dating clients. You know that."

The guy-liner voice was sexy and low. However, the thick, dark smudges weren't guy-liner, they were totally just the lashes that were brimming this guy's peepers.

"Have you heard a word I've said?" Claire waved her hands in front of Hazel's face.

Hazel grabbed them and held them. "No. I was eavesdropping."

Claire followed Hazel's gesture and saw Gaston and Dark Lashes having heated words. "I might have to write that up as some fan-fiction with me in the middle."

Hazel laughed. "I think I'd read the hell out of that."

Dark Lashes stalked away, and Hazel got a glimpse of his tight ass. He even had a tattoo trailing up his forearm.

"You're checking him out, aren't ya?" Claire slipped her arm around Hazel's waist.

"I'm scoping this joint out so when they start swearing us in to the cult, I know how to get us out." Hazel wrapped her arm around Claire as well and felt the tips of her friend's long red hair brush her skin.

"So cynical. Seriously, we've watched the ads a million times.

A hundred and ten percent guaranteed to find your soul mate. I mean, how can we not take the chance? Did I tell you that's his name, too? Chance." Claire wiggled the tips of her fingertips in Gaston's direction. He *would* be named Chance.

"I'm going to take a Chance right in the back of my throat if he gives a girl a shot. Damn. Have we ever met someone so incredibly big? He's like a house. Do you see the way his T-shirt looks like it's going to tear right off his goddamned body?"

Hazel tried to find Dark Lashes, but he was gone. Instead, she was meeting all kinds of inquisitive eyes from the other men in the lobby. It was a meat market.

"He should have gotten the next size up. One sneeze and he'll tear right out of his clothes."

"A girl can hope. Do you have pepper in your purse?" Claire seemed serious as she pawed at Hazel's bag.

"No. Stop. We have to listen." The teacher in Hazel insisted on paying attention when someone was trying to speak to a group.

When Claire saw that it was Chance clapping, she was instantly riveted and stopped trying to mug Hazel.

It took a few claps and a whistle or two, but eventually the singles were eyes forward.

"Welcome to Booty Camp Dating Service!" Chance totally defeated all his efforts to quiet the crowd with his boisterous greeting. The crowd hooted and clapped.

Booty Camp Dating Service was so aggressively advertised on TV, on social media, and on billboards it almost seemed like they were meeting a celebrity. Well, if the celebrity was a dating app. It toured the United States, and there had been a marked increase in births roughly nine months after they'd embarked on the first leg.

Despite the cheeky name, Booty Camp Dating Service had a stupidly fabulous reputation for matching singles with their forever person. It had reached epic proportions, especially with late-night TV doing skits about Booty Camp.

The classically opulent theater was a study in deep red velvets and gold trimmings. Booty Camp was in town for two months. And Booty Camp was expensive. After winning the ticket lotto —thanks to Claire for babysitting that process without saying a word—Hazel was rewarded with having to lay out a thousand dollars for the honor of becoming a coveted Booty Camp success story. A hundred and ten percent happy. That's what the ads all said, anyway.

Chance managed to get the crowd settled again.

"Congrats on your admission to the program! We're so successful because *you* will be successful. After you've been processed by one of our Booty professionals, please make your way into the screening room."

Quite a few girls around them were fanning their faces and sneaking snapshots on their phone of Chance beef-caking around. The doors were opened by Booty Camp counselors.

Dark Lashes was hanging back, and Hazel pretended to sweep her hair up to a ponytail and peeked over her shoulder at him at the same time.

He caught her eye and gave her a very fatherly wink. She bit her lip so she wouldn't frown.

Claire nudged her. "Let's go. I want to get a good seat. Why are you blushing?"

"No reason. This whole thing makes me self-conscious."

The theater was well-lit and had deep, velvet seats. The pushier among the group made their way to the front, closest to the stage and, therefore, the screen. It was as if these people thought getting the best seats would help them find their soul mates quicker. Hazel pulled on Claire's arm until they were in the center of the back row.

Claire wiggled in her seat when Chance found her and pointed at her from the stage where he now stood, holding a microphone. After everyone was seated and the excitement had died down, Chance stirred them up again.

"Your soul mate could be here. Right now." He motioned around the packed theater. "Look around. It's not uncommon for our Booty Camp clients to lock eyes right this moment with the person they'll marry in six months. So do it. Feel it."

Hazel could feel her eyes rolling, so she closed them in case—on some random chance—the man for her was here, his first vision of her wouldn't be filled with the sarcasm. It felt like a superstition or an exercise in fruition. But she didn't throw out a raffle ticket until the numbers were announced, either, so...

She looked over her shoulder and found herself staring at Dark Lashes. He didn't smile, and neither did she. He looked bored. Like just another day at the office, which she guessed it was for him as he sat in the back row adjacent to hers. Finally, he touched his temple with his index finger and pointed back at the crowd in front of them. It took her a minute to understand his sign language, but when she got it, she felt her cheeks flush. He wanted her to put her gaze forward. To stop looking at him.

She bit her bottom lip. What an asshole. What did he think— she was trying to tempt him into dating her?

Hazel gave him the middle finger and an exasperated look. He could jump to conclusions, but she wasn't here to try and snag a man. Well, she wouldn't mind finding a guy to take back to her apartment so Scott would have to step around them making out in front of the elevator. That would be some sweet revenge.

She gave Dark Lashes another hard look, and this time he seemed to be struggling with a smirk.

"Jerk," Hazel muttered.

"Who? Chance?" Claire was focused on the man on stage who was feeding the crowd some impossible statistics.

"Did you know that woman who are single after twenty- six

244

are eighty-nine percent more likely to die alone than their dating counterparts?" Chance stalked to the edge of the stage and fake whispered into the mic, "And men who don't settle down see a reduction in penis length at the rate of three centimeters a year after forty if they haven't found a permanent partner?"

"None of that is true. He's making that up," Claire said while Hazel gave Lashes another stare. He didn't seem alarmed at the wild accusations Chance was slinging.

"Do those facts scare you? I hope you know they're false. As far as I know, anyway."

Claire leaned in and whispered, "See?" in Hazel's ear.

"That's what the media wants you to believe. They try to shame you into finding love. And here at Booty Camp, we want to tell you we're here for a great reason. It's okay to be single. It's okay to be satisfied with your life on your own. We just happen to know that that's not your feelings. No one pays a thousand dollars because they want to be alone."

Claire and Hazel looked at each other. Claire mouthed, "Well, *maybe you* do," which prompted Hazel to punch the top of her friend's arm.

"There is the desire to find a match, but at Booty Camp, we believe in destiny. That you are put on a path to lead you somewhere in particular."

Chance stooped lower and spoke to the first row like he was in a hair band in the 80s.

"Our competitors will say that if you have enough matching interests, you can get together and make a go of this crazy world. And that may be true, but here at Booty Camp, we want you to find The One. Your Happily Ever After. The prince, or princess, of your dreams. We believe in one true love for every person. That's why we're better. You *will* find your other half. The apple to your peach. The butter on your toast. We seek perfection. And we find it."

Chance delivered the last lines straight to Claire. The whole room must have felt the chemistry between them because people turned and craned their necks to see who, exactly, had inspired that level of intensity from the speaker. Claire's lips were opened slightly, almost breathlessly. She reached for Hazel's hand and squeezed it like they were about to go down the scariest hill on a roller coaster together.

Claire looked so enchanted it was like she was acting in a movie.

She kept her eyes on the speaker, but spoke quietly to Hazel. "I'm going to marry that man."

Hazel's mouth dropped open.

READ MORE HERE: https://amzn.to/3MkyTMF

ABOUT THE AUTHOR

Debra creates pretend people in her head and paints them on the giant, beautiful canvas of your imagination. She has a Bachelor of Science degree in political science and writes new adult angst and romantic comedies. She lives in Maryland with her husband and two amazing children. She doesn't trust mannequins, but does trust bears. Also, her chunk tuxedo cat talks with communication buttons. So that's fun. DebraAnastasia.com for more information.

Pretty please review this book if you enjoyed it. It is one of the very best ways to support indy authors. Thank you! (Plus, anyone that reviews is granted three wishes by the first unicorn they meet.)

ALSO BY DEBRA ANASTASIA

Angst with Feels:

DROWNING IN STARS

STEALING THE STARS

https://www.debraanastasia.com/drowing-in-stars-giveaway

Mafia Romance:

MERCY

HAVOC

LOCK

https://www.debraanastasia.com/mercy-verse

Silly Humor:

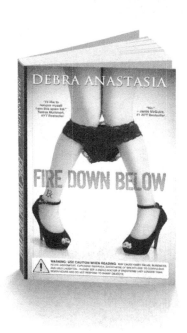

FIRE DOWN BELOW

FIRE IN THE HOLE

https://www.debraanastasia.com/humor

Funny Humor:

FLICKER

BEAST

BOOTY CAMP

FELONY EVER AFTER

https://www.debraanastasia.com/more-humor

Paranormal:

THE REVENGER

FOR ALL THE EVERS

CRUSHED SERAPHIM (BOOK 1)

https://www.debraanastasia.com/paranormal

FREE BOOK PLATES

Okay Daredevils. I have literally the cutest offer ever for you. My dad makes my swag down in Florida. He is freaking adorable about it and is very serious about his job. If you want a FREE signed bookplate(s) email my dad and we will send them to you and whatever swag he can fit in the envelope.

To receive an envelope sealed with adorableness and extreme efficiency email: debraanastasiaDad@gmail.com with your full name and mailing address (plus how many bookplates you need!!)

ACKNOWLEDGMENTS

A huge thanks to you, the reader. I am so honored to get to visit your imagination again. I published my first book on 2011. How time flies. You've let so many characters into your heart, and I'm so excited to bring you many more. I hope this note finds you well and happy.

To my beautiful family, T, J and D, I absolutely adore you and am so proud of all of you. Thank you for putting up with me.

A HUGE shout out to my parents, Steve and Valerie. Dad A has become a celebrity for his adorable swag envelopes and birthday cards he sends out to readers. Mom A is in charge of sparkle and glitter. They support everything I do and then some. Pam and Jim! Thanks for keeping my bedroom ready in NY I love you. To Jim's mom Cathy, you are incredible.

Helena Hunting, I'm so glad you haven't figured out that you got the short end of the deal in this extensive friendship. I wouldn't want to do this without you.

Tijan, my mystical bad ass friend. Thank you for being so positive all the time. You are fantastic.

Mom and Dad D, you are gifts, and I am so lucky to have you.

Amanda Rush Proofreading for the most elegant proof in the world.

All my Beta Beauties! Michele, Marty and Brandi, Amanda, Carol S! You are an emergency swat time of awesome.

Sweet Gel! All the beautiful pictures!

Debra's Daredevils! We've been doing this for so long, I am the luckiest.

Whole Brower Literary Crew—Amiee Ashcraft and Kimberly Brower Thank you so much for everything!

Aunt Jo and Uncle Ted—you guys are so cool.

BLACKBERRY the talking cat.

Buds: Erika, you are the best

Christina Santos always

Cassie S thank you so much for all your help

Sara from Enchanting Romance Designs

Paige Smith Editing

Kelly B, Ashley S, LLL, Sarah Pie,

Social Butterfly PR

Made in the USA
Monee, IL
21 May 2022

96804570R00144